LOOKING AT THE WALL

Anima Chakraverty

First published in 2020 by

Becomeshakespeare.com

One Point Six Technologies Pvt. Ltd.
Unit - 26, Building A -1, Nr Wadala RTO,
Wadala (East), Mumbai 400037, India
T: +91 8080226699

Copyrights © by Anima Chakraverty

Internal illustrator: Anirvan Roy
Cover Designer: Ami Parekh

ISBN 978-93-90543-22-9

ABOUT THE AUTHOR

Anima Chakraverty has taught for over a decade. She has a large number of publications and presentations to her credit, with two National awards for innovative practices in teaching and for teaching short stories.

ACKNOWLEDGEMENTS

I dedicate this work to my parents Dr. S.N. & Mrs. Savitri Chakraverty; Ma and Pa Your love and persistent support helped me find my own voice. My sisters Mrs. Protima Mukherjee, Dr. Kolpona Werner and their families' for their patience.

To my extended family Dr. Devika Nag for having to read the stories and give her opinion. To Ms. Shikhi Sharma prodding me to finish.

I would like to earnestly thank the following for their sincere efforts and their valuable time:

Internal illustrator: Anirvan Roy

Project Manager: Shreyas Prathamshetti

Cover designer: Ami Parekh

Team from One Point Six Technologies Pvt. Ltd.

We read short stories simply because we like it. We like it because it is an image of life, it stimulates and gratifies our interest in life.

A short story like other works of fiction is not hundred percent real life account, but a product of the author's imagination, though it may have risen from an experience. Stories have a wide range of subjects. The only limit on a story is its length. A short story must be readable in one sitting. A good short story presents enough life like qualities to help us better understand our self's and our world.

The stories are grouped according to some basic elements that an author works with when writing a story. The key to approaching any story with deeper understanding gives greater pleasure.

What happens in a short story can be sketched in a few words But, the bare outline is not interesting without the rich details that give a story colour, life, complication and meaning.

The book 'Looking at the Wall' is in two parts. The first set of stories are traditional and satisfy one who's looking for a rounding off. The second set leaves a lot to the imagination. It plays with the thought of the reader. Understanding the stories means paying attention to the details. If we pay attention to these details, we will be amply rewarded in the pleasure we gain from careful reading.

Happy thoughtful Reading.

CONTENTS

PART- I

Part- I

GRANDMOTHER'S FOOTSTEPS

Grandmother had worked hard all her life. Still strong. Still stubborn. Her eyes now softened, as if in forced compromise. Contemplating on how far she had come.

She sat reclining in her old arm chair, in the open balcony, enjoying the partial rays of the sun. In this position she could see from the corner of her eye, that he still seemed absorbed in writing. From that distance she couldn't make out, if the paper spread around had anything written on it. Yet, he had a pen in hand, and gazed out of the open window.

From that distance she wondered, how her Ajju looked? Surely, something must have happened. Ever since he has returned from Ira's, he has been at a loss. She felt like getting up and going quietly to him. She wanted to put her hand on his back and express her affection, and take his face in her hands, turn it towards her and ask "Ajju, what has happened to you?"

But, a young grandson, now, where was the close relationship, that she could with ease ask him any personal question, and expect a straight answer? She hesitated in approaching him, as if he was not her own grandson, but a strange man. When did this communication barrier come between them? This is a mystery. This was her little Ajju, whom she had mothered. For years she had cleaned him and bathed him and today she was so afraid to ask him a simple question.

Even last time when he lost his job he was quite for a long time. Then he did not say a word to her. She got to know from Ira and his other friends, that he had, had a misunderstanding with the boss and had given up his job. There was so much turmoil in his mind – what could have happened that the relationship between him and his boss snapped so suddenly. There was a special rapport between them. It was Ira who had told her then. "Grandma, he was so close to them, that he had no independence to work. How long could he remain their puppet? You don't know, but it is harmful, to come too close in a work relationship. Familiarity always breeds contempt."

Then too she had wanted to ask Ira, hasn't your relationship come very close too? What results will it have, lass?

She was not able to understand their relationship. She had been seeing Ira in and out of the house for the past seven years. Sometimes she came alone, at other times with Ajju and their friends. In a big city she lived all alone. Without either parent, brother or sister, she had taken a flat. Sometimes Ajjay remained away from home for days. He would give her, Ira's phone number, he was under the same roof. They openly accepted their liking for each other. But marriage? No, not for them yet. They were testing whether they could get along or not.

What is love? What is testing? She could not understand this even after her entire life. When she was still playing with her friends, she was given away in marriage to some stranger. She was the bride, and a husband good or bad, was God on earth. This was her belief. That is how she had looked at him till she was widowed. She was religiously regular in carrying out rituals and fasts, for the long life of her husband. One never thought a woman can have any dilemma in giving herself physically to her husband, whenever he demanded. To bring up the children and to take care of the home was slavery or duty? She never knew the difference nor did she question it.

Today, this Ira and Ajjay.

From where do they get topics for their long discussion. On what issues to they argue, what sadness and loneliness fill his stories. And this Ira, what absurd pictures does she keeping making? She says she expresses a woman's deepest and finest emotions in her pictures. Once she had taken me to see an exhibition of her paintings. A large hall covered with large pictures. Women in numerous forms. In all unique angles possible.

Women standing at an angle (Oh the pressure!). Women drowning-floating, women turned upside down, hanging from the sky, women ready to fly with wings nipped, bird like women, women with animal horns and eyes, sensual women, women powerful like Durga, women ruthless, strong and destructive like Kali, only women and women.

Have women become so important in today's world?

You will not understand mother, the woman of your time inhaled subjugation from men. Man had thus mesmerized them. Man had overpowered women with his physical and emotional demands, and women totally lost themselves. Yet everything was getting on fine.

Was it really getting on? Dissatisfied women with unfulfilled desires. Women restless to get, what they did not get from their husbands. What is this – news of bride burning? Is it the anger of suppressed and harassed women, after all what is it? "So, your generation is luckier. Now that you are independent to do what you want; you must be pleased."

"My generation? Independent? The fate of women is not going to change for one or two generations. Mother, from whom we are going to get this independence? It is all outward show. What kind of independence. Independence indeed! How is it possible till man does not change his attitude?" Smiling ironically, she gave her hand, leading her forward.

"Come look at this painting, it is of Ahalya. Do you know what Ahalya stands for? An emotionally and physically deprived woman. A dissatisfied woman whose emotional and physical growth is stunted. Circumstances have changed her. She has become feelingless and hard like stone. This is all because she has waited in vain for her ideal man, one who can arouse the woman in her."

"Ideal Man?"

She only knew a man, one man, in the form of husband; whether he is ideal or not never entered her thoughts. He is the man, she is the woman, and that is sufficient. When did one ever think of physically or mental desires, did anyone try to know her desire? Nor was there any communication on the subject. She was never thought capable of it. Under cover of darkness he would come and claim her as if it was his right, and leave. That a woman too can claim physical bliss was not even dreamt of. Yes, awareness of physical desires was surely there. My brother-in-law, two years younger than me, when taking the store room keys, or accepting a glass of lassi, would definitely touch my fingers. What sensation would arise in me, large wanton eyes, curly hair, how appealing he looked, so many times she wanted ....! Shame accused her conscience, it was a sin to think of any other man but one's husband, but what to do with real dreams? It was in her dreams only that she realized that she was turned off from Ajju's grandfather. What controls can one have over dreams. How many times did she see Nicky in her dreams, bent over her, with such warmth, with such affection, as if worshipping her, and when she opened her eyes Oh! How guilty she was. She was covered in perspiration. Even though that had been a dream, she felt as if she had sinned. She would be ashamed of herself all day, in case anyone got to know.

Now this Ira. She is not even ashamed or scared of anyone.

The first time I saw her I was surprised by her behaviour. Glancing casually at me, without even a greeting, Ira walked past. A lit cigarette in hand she walked into Ajju's room, as if I was a ghost, some redundant commodity. Probably, Ajju had not mentioned me to her. Anyway, Ajju didn't seem to care, whether she existed or not. At that age despite all her physical infirmities, she was managing Ajju's house, because he was her grandson. But he didn't understand his responsibilities, was this how one behaved with one's elders? Men have one way of looking at women. If their behaviour is rational it can be understood. A man should get married and establish his home. But if you even ask, the prompt reply is, what's the hurry?

Ira is in the house all day, as if it's hers, why doesn't he bring her to the house respectfully and legally. She will have no objections. Now even Ira had started liking her. She would even come in Ajju's absence to be with her. Ira had opened up so much, she had been confiding in her and talking to her as a friend. You won't believe it, I was extremely simple to the verge of being foolish, when I got married, I hadn't completed eighteen. My parents saw the family, his good position and consented, and tied me to him so that he may not slip out of their hands, could he let me do what I wanted. At my father's house I had flitted around like a butterfly, nothing was refused, nor were there any rules for me. But there I had to be extraordinarily cautious; today I couldn't do this and tomorrow that; all the traditions and customs were for me. On one side the in-laws dictating, and on the other the husband's demands whenever he wanted. To tell the truth I hated him. But I tolerated everything. However, when he raised his hand on me, I returned home. And once I returned there was no going back. He moved the divorce papers, he came and got it signed. So finally, I was rid of him. There was only one regret that I had no child.

There is a limit to shamelessness!

Last week when she came, she sat on the ground and put her head on my knees. Then she took my hand in her's and looking into my eyes said, I have created a new painting, of a woman. She often talked in riddles, but the way she said one of my wishes has come true.

She had her doubts from the beginning observing her movements; surprised she stared at her, she was not ashamed in saying, but she was hesitant in asking if it was Ajju's. However, taking courage, when Ajju returned home she asked him.

Was it fated to tolerate all this in one's old age from one's youngsters? Yet she consoled herself, whatever it is the girl is not too bad, she cared for her. Where one has adjusted to changing time, this too is a part of it. Ajju is probably hesitant to speak up himself. So, she advised him to get married soon.

She prompted Ajju and sent him to Ira's. At this time, poor thing, she needs support and reassurance. Even if it is an Aryasamaj marriage, they should have a small function, and she'll bring her daughter-in-law home. Climbing and descending stairs has become too painful, so I don't come down anymore, otherwise I would have gone to Ira myself.

One by one all her jewelry had been presented. The last that remained was a necklace. Putting it in Ajju's hand she said, "give this to your wife from me." After having gone yesterday, Ajju returned this morning. Ever since he had bee sitting at the table. When he writes he doesn't like disturbance? But is he really writing?

On returning he did not even tell her what the conversation with Ira had been. What was her reaction after seeing the necklace? When is she coming to meet her? What will she do with her flat? Many thoughts entered her mind. But this grandson of hers, what kind of writer was he?

Her heart melts seeing Ajju. Now definitely something is the matter. She can no longer sit and watch. What happened at Ira's place that….? Can there be a possibility of any misunderstanding, any disappointment…? Oh! This pain in my knees. Once she sits it is difficult to get up. Resting her arm on the arm of the chair she gradually gets up.

She turned towards his room. Resting his head on the back of his chair, he had shut his eyes. She was filled with concern. In spite her weakness, she walked towards Ajju. On hearing her footsteps, he suddenly broke out of his reverie and saw her in front of him.

What happened Grandma? She wasn't expecting to confront him from so close. With slight hesitation she asked "What happened ……. What happened to you that ……...? He stood up. Probably, he had never thought of facing her so directly, looking down in embarrassment he said, "Grandma, you will not understand."

Then immediately he pulled the drawer of his table and took out his car keys. Putting his hand into his kurta pocket, as if searching, he took out something, throwing it on the table he said, "She has returned this……."

He hurriedly tried to leave the room, before closing the door he turned and shouted, "Says the child is only her's, ONLY HER'S. That I should not try to make any claims— Bloody Bitch! She is not a woman but a stone statue." Shocked she stared at vacant chair, clutching it she saw him leave.

She was torn to pieces, pained for whom she did not know. "Don't I understand? I understand everything, you as well as her. How can I blame her coldness, and her hardness? He hasn't been able to awaken the woman in her by being her ideal man."

LONGING

I am eighteen and my dress fascinates me. This, however, does not mean that I am pleased with it, mind you, or that I can even tolerate it. I, simply am interested in dressing.

Each day I look someone different. I never know what it's going to be like, until I steal a look at the mirror. Oh! I don't suppose you can call it stealing. It belongs to me after all.

One day I look sophisticated in a raw rust silk with extravagant accessories and the aura of Channel 5 in the air. On the other, an elite collegian with jeans, a T-shirt and a jacket, a transformed person. On the third, a fair sex in her mini skirt, with a deep neckline and fancy boots. On the fourth day, I honour the youthful tradition of grace. A long neat kamiz, flowing chunni with a salwar that can be alternated by a churidar if the occasion demands. And a change from sober fawn, to deep hues of brown, to be transformed into a neat gray. More so, when the need demands overnight. So much so that I can turn around and tell the onlooker……… "My dress is my fortune."

Some morning if I look at the mirror soon after getting out of bed, there is no resemblance of me in either of my outfits, and I turn to look behind me, convinced that a stranger has spent the night with me and is peering from behind, in a sinister fashion, merely to frighten me. On such an occasion, the shock of finding that I am the actual possessor of the face in the mirror and not the variety of dress, is sufficient to send me scurrying back to bed, completely unnerved.

All this of course, is very depressing and I often give off a low moan at the sight of a new day's metamorphose, but I can seem to resist the temptation to learn the worst. I even go out of my way to look at myself at store windows, just to see how long it takes me to recognize myself, if I happen to have on a new jumpsuit or a flowing hand pleated skirt. I walk past my reflection without even nodding. Then I begin to think "You must have given off some visual impression into the mirror. You are not a disembodied spirit yet–I hope."

I go back and look again and sure enough the strange looking individual I thought was ahead of me; the reflection turns out to have been my own image all the time. This is a most masochistic craving to offend my own aesthetic sense by looking at myself and wincing at photographs.   I surreptitiously go through, the one in which I show up nicely just to gaze my fill on a slightly macabre sight of myself as others see me.

But day in and day out, in the mirror,   there is always that shock, which although unpleasant, lends a tang to adventure. I can never make it quite possible that, 'Poor little me', the little me I know so well and yet who frightens me when face to face.

My own hope in the metamorphosis, which seems to be going on, is that it may bring a winning number someday. But whatever is in store for me, I shall watch the daily modulation that a dress can bring about, with an impersonal fascination not unmixed with awe.

LEAVE THE DOOR UNBOLTED

"Leave that door alone, young man and remember once and for all that it's never to be locked or bolted. Not that there's any fear of its being locked, as the master always has the key on him."

Mrs. Mani heard the muffled worlds. Ramu, their seventy-year old servant, instructed the new recruit, in impressive tones, serious when addressing his humble subordinate. "That's funny"! "It may be funny to you, a stranger, Kalu, but it's only a sad one to me. "Sad? Why's that Ramu?"

By then Mrs. Mani had reached the door of her bedroom, she heard a quivering familiar old voice answer "T" was this the way it happened. Rakesh was a rare young chap, he was, not just put down as killed, when he didn't come back from camp. He was just reported missing. Cruel, I called it then and cruel, I call it now for it was bound to encourage false hopes".

Mrs., Mani knew well enough what missing meant. But the master, he just couldn't bring himself to believe his son, his heir, had gone, so to speak forever. "I remember well, how a few days after the incident, Mr. Mani came along one night as I was locking up, and he said, "Just leave the door of the hall as it is, Ramu. Rakesh always came into the house that way, because of the short cut from the gate. My son may walk back through the same door one day." That's what he said, "poor gentleman, and that door, Kalu, has never been locked since."

The men walked their way. Mrs. Mani thought, "How strange that she should not have known, till that night, of her husband's order. It was true that all ages past boyhood, the boy had wanted to burst through the outer door off what was called the hall, with a cry "Mother, where are you?" "Upstairs." And yet, dearly as he loved her, close as they were to one another, she had known Rakesh had cared more for his father.

She has so moved, now, that something of a frightful anguish of six years ago came back and restlessly she began to walk up and down the beautiful bedroom envied by many of her friends. How terrible that to her it should be a room of intolerable memories.

In this wide bed, where she now spent her often wakeful nights, had been born their son. How often, in the last six years, she had wished she die on that glorious day her son was born. Suddenly, she stopped pacing opposite a carved wooden mirror. She had been standing just there during her last happy moments of life. At exactly three o'clock there was a knock on the door. Blithely she had called out, "Come in."

And he had come in, with a telegram open in his hand. It was as if she could hear now, tonight six years later, the sounds of his hoarse voice uttering her name and then when she had put up her arm with an instinctive violent movement to ward off the blow, the further words, Thank God not killed only "missing."

Only missing? And Rakesh's father had gone on, not only hoping against hope, just firmly convinced that the boy would come back.

She, from the beginning in dry-eyed despair, had felt no hope at all. And her husband's obstinacy, what she recognized, as idiotic optimism, had pained, exasperated and sometimes maddened her. And now while slowly undressing, she wondered with a touch of unease, if her husband was unhappy as she was herself. Unlocking the drawers in which lay all the photographs of Rakesh, she took out the last one, while she gazed into the boyish face, he seemed to be smiling proudly, confidently, and merrily up at her. And in this way, she sat remembering. When–

The twelfth stroke of the clock fell on the still air and all at once she heard the electric light being turned out in the hall below, followed by the sound of her husband's odd unexpected footsteps. She wanted to go out and bid him goodnight, but she restrained that impulse. All the same she walked across to the door and turning off the light, noiselessly, opened it a little.

Mr. Mani was making his way up the stairs with the steps of an old man, though she knew he was still young at heart. And still feeling moved by what their old servant had unconsciously revealed, she waited to hear those slow footsteps make their way to the room.

And then as if her heart stood still, for the handle of the unbolted door in the hall below, turned in the darkness, and there came an upward rush of cold air, followed by her husband's shout: "Who's there?" There was moment's pause, and after that pause, as if from infinitely far away, there rang out two words, in a voice, she had never thought she would hear again. And these words uttered in her sons' voice pierced her innermost soul, for 'Poor father' was all her beloved had come back to say. Then she heard Mr. Mani eager and joyful, "Rakesh! my dear boy" and the sound of his feet pounding down the stairs.

And as she rushed out in the circular gallery, she heard the handle turn again in the darkness. The lights below were switched on and looking over the banister, she saw her husband standing in the empty hall, staring with bewildered eyes at the closed door. At last he turned, and looking up, saw her pale face and wide open eyes gazing down. "You heard him too?"

Straightening herself she ran down the stairs. There with what had become a way of forgotten tenderness she took his hand– "Of course I heard him too. The door opened and he came in with the wind. Having said what was in his mind he went back, but where, where–"

Later that night Rakesh's father muttered, "he came back for you, to comfort you. That was quite right."

"For me? Oh no!"

"But he did, surely you heard what he said?" and she felt the surprise in his voice. She whispered, "What did he say to you?"

'Only what you heard, the two words. DEAR MOTHER". He waited a moment and then he said, in a mumble, for he was a simple, kind man. "Just to let you know and perhaps, to let me know, too, that all is well."

STRIKINGLY PLAIN

Rasika, was not beautiful, yet striking. Average in height. Favored with a healthy build, with all her curves in the right place. Her shy, serious smile, square determined chin offset her large dove-like eyes. Anyone wishing to know her a little closer, had better hurry before she took flight! Eager to share her youth and warmth, before the journey ran out. Exploring too, the adage Rasika had created for herself, "If one is to become beautiful, beauty has to shine from within."

She was now flowering into womanhood, her thoughts turning towards settling down by getting married to a-well-to-do-man. Her parents, too, are one with her decision. And belonging to a conventional, middle-class family, Rasika's parents are going to choose her groom. The Times of India, a popular newspaper with the matrimonial was their best guide. After a thorough search, through the columns, they came across an advertisement that read:

"WANTED A SWEET DISPOSITIONED, MODERN HOMELY GIRL, FOR A WELL-SETTLED BANK EXECUTIVE. NO DEMANDS."

Correspondence began progressing well. A mutual and satisfactory meeting was arranged by the respective parents, where the usual formal courtesies and friendliness exchanged. Rasika's father was as hospitable and gracious as ever.

In the traditional style, the girl is shown and the terms were agreed upon. Somehow, the situation created a feeling of disgust in Rasika. As if, she was on parade. Dressed, to kill. When she had a display a false shyness that really made her feel foolish—killing the real Rasika. Yet? Yet, both set of parents kept talking. Deciding that the youngsters should meet. But, first Mr. Pandey, decides to talk to Rasika.

Rasika, was certainly a young woman who could think for herself. Witty, and well-informed. The forthcoming meeting with Mr. Pandey, her prospective father-in-law, held high anticipation.

Rasika, at Mr. Pandey's library, she taps shyly on his door, "May I come in please?" Mr. Pandey, looks up and replies, "Yes, do". As she walks towards him Rasika is carefully studied. Nearing him, she respectfully greets him, "Good Morning."

"Good morning", Mr. Pandey, trying not to look at Rasika too intently, remembering to ask her to, "Take a seat, please". Quickly rising from his own, exchanging a steel chair with one that was more comfortable, equally trying very hard not to sound to patronizing. "Wait a minute, let me get you another, this one would be too inconvenient". Rasika quickly sits down, opting for the steel chair gracefully, smiles, "No thanks. This one is perfectly all right." Mr. Pandey's eyebrows arch and then, he smiles gently, taking a seat opposite her, "I thought, girls, were supposed to be, eh?

A half-smile, "Physically delicate and weak. So, I wanted to get you something more comfortable." Rasika shifts a little, dispersing her irritation. "Thank you. But, I hope, you're not trying to make me feel inferior to a man? She said, with a smile." His embarrassment, Throwing calmly the question to her, "You think you are as good and strong as a man? in every walk of life , "Why?" Adding a little honey to a hornet's nest, "were not women conscious of their potential, in the past?" Continuing, respectfully, seeing another slight twitch in Mr. Pandey's eyebrow. Placing her raven- hair over her shoulders, she exclaimed, "Mainly, because psychologically, we were always made to feel inferior and if people are made to feel this way about themselves, then you become so. We see every change, of course, for the better, for women these days." Rasika, spontaneously, added with a laugh, "And I believed, you, (looking at Mr. Pandey) you wouldn't be envious of such progress!" Even if I am", Mr. Pandey turns his palm to the ceiling. "I could not really stop the storm women are releasing all around the world."

"I believe, you are from Bihar?" asked Mr. Pandey. "No" Rasika answers politely, lowering her voice. "I am from U.P." "So, you are an UPite?" "Neither, an UPite nor, a Behari?" Then   ?" Mr. Pandey, wanted to ask Rasika -

– "What, are you? Where, are you from? A southern wind, which suddenly has a northern bite?" He refrained however.

This angered Rasika, somewhat, but, she did not show it. Instead, she said as nicely as possible, I'm a human being, of course! And I'm meant to be in the community you belong to. Somehow, my mind did not transcend artificial barriers. Or, which aren't there. To me, human society is one and indivisible."

'Your thoughts?" Mr. Pandey, paused, as if he was analyzing his own. Even partly, for Rasika – how she had revealed herself" Your thoughts, are indeed good. Reflecting your ideas, clearly. "What?" Hesitantly, and yet, eagerly to find out. "What do you think should be a relationship between a husband and wife?" Truthful, or perhaps, in a half-truth, Rasika, chose her words carefully, – "Well, I haven't given it much thought. But I feel a relationship between husband wife should be on mutual cooperation. A spirit of give-and- take, as equal partners in a joint journey which, we call the family.

Mr. Pandey, resting back on his chair, placing his praying finger-tips near his mouth, looking with an earnest smile at Rasika, "Will you marry man who demands a dowry?" "Franky speaking, my marrying such a man, or should I say, if ever I should find myself in such a position, right from the start will frustrate a happy marriage."

Mr. Pandey, "How will you react if, you are not selected? Candidly, Rasika, said, "In Indian homes, men decide and women have to accept. But I am not pessimistic. Hopefully, my decisions do not depend on, "ifs". She smiled her most charming smile, 'I have always been hopeful. If rejection comes, I hope I will be resolute enough to face whatever is before me."

As if he was leading a lamb to slaughter, Mr. Pandey asked, "Would you like a pursue a career, after you are married? Or, would you be content with just a family life? What kind of work would you like to do?"

Rasika, still retaining her individuality, politely answered,

"One of the ways for a woman to find herself and come to know who she is, is through work of her own. Having a profession equal cannot only be stretching but essential to inspire an interest or a goal, outside the home for some part of the day. Of course, I will enjoy being a housewife. Though falling into this trap, isn't something I would readily do. As everybody, I need to work to eat. But it's my identity I value and this is going to feed the survival of my soul, which will give me a really sense of being in society."

Mr. Pandey exclaimed, "Rasika! How can you talk that way? Women are meant to be married! Have children and make their husbands happy." One would think, this statement, as a fact of life—would take Rasika's breath away. It did for a bit. Though, as an actress speaking her part to an unseen camera, she said calmly, "I don't think I would like to marry, becoming a man's domestic pet. To be treated like a child, without a mind of my own. Having all my movements, my finances controlled. Why! I'd rather be dead."

Getting interested, Mr. Pandey leaned forward and asked quietly – "And what is this trap, Rasika, you speak about?" "Why! The common problem that practically all women experience." Rasika, still searching for the right words. "Oh, if you would like to know", she exploded with a desperate sigh, "I don't want to be—a victim of some deadly boring routine. To see life loose its personal quest for ME. I have a heart. I would like to marry the 'right man. Have 'our' children. My heart, though, also seeks a place of giving, and growth in the rest of the world which is my world as well as yours. Once, women marry, you must agree, women, as a rule, loose a sense of who they are and I don't want that."

Mr. Pandey, cleared his throat with irritation and disappointment. Smiling a fixed smile and rubbing the side of his cheek, thoughtfully, he took her hand in his, standing, to shake it, saying, "Well, Rasika, I have really enjoyed this talk with you. You indeed, have taught me a lot."

Alone in his library, Mr. Pandey, seriously recapped his conversation with Rasika. Such a modern, educated young woman. She, was certainly a surprise! Most appealing. He, although, couldn't see eye to eye, with her…. With such a rebellious streak, with her face covered and head bowed as a docile bride and wife, looking after one of his sons. Washing, cleaning, cooking–answering demands. Forgetting, her own completely.

However, With a distant or future shine in his eye, Mr. Pandey leans across the list on his desk and neatly crosses off Rasika's name. Rasika is rejected as a daughter-in-law. But, as for rejecting herself? Even Mr. Pandey, couldn't see this being possible! Striking back, she certainly could!

SORROW'S CROWN OF SORROWS

Two, three, four months and hopelessness all around. No signs of an appointment. Not even a call letter. Disapprovals had gradually seemed to pile up. As a result, I was habitually despondent; contemplating that luck was always against me. Yet the last hope was to sit for a competition.

The usual preparation started. My friend found me sweating away as usual. Often, she wondered what I was up to. To her invitation 'Hello, come out, shut your old books, and come and play a game of tennis. 'I'd reply, 'I'm sorry, I can't do that. The examination is drawing near and I want every hour I can get for study. "Oh! hang all examination. I do not worry about mine, what is the use of them anyway?"

Well if you can't pass an examination, you can't get a job and I have set my heart on one. I tell you, all one needs to get on in the world is some brains, plain common sense and plenty of push. And you can't learn these things from books. Yet, I was persistent. Hope made me plod on. Finally, I took the examination A few days and the result will be announced. Waiting with dim hope had made me pale with anxiety.

Ultimately, the day dawned and gloomy dark clouds encircled me. Amidst thunder and lightning the wind roared and the rain poured.

Disappointment seemed around the corner. I sat silent, waiting patiently. A friend with a practical turn of mind sat by me, as if one with me in my anxiety. The hour came and the news struck me.

Grave silence followed. Undisturbed for what seemed a long time, hope seemed to have ebbed completely out of me. I sat lifeless. Alas, the sound of my friend's voice woke me from the trauma. "Come, come you are taking your failure too much to heart. I understand, and I sympathize with you, but you must not allow it to make you so unhappy. There is no pleasure without pain. Life has its ups and downs with everyone. One must learn to accept misfortune as they come. Moreover, everything happens for the best." I gather courage and in my meek voice expressed myself. The shock had shaken me. And the best way, to overcome it was to express it. Bitterness should not be allowed to penetrate, grow and mature in one's mind. It is the most destructive feeling one can nurture.

"It's all very well for a lucky girl like you, Meeta. You have qualified in the first go, and this is my second failure. You would not feel so cheerful if you were in my place." "I realize, but you must pull yourself together and make up your mind, you will pass next time. Remember the age old saying? It stands good even today…If at first you don't succeed, try, try, and try again."

Reluctantly I whispered, "I think the other version of the saying is 'If you don't succeed quit, quit and quit at once.' My heart was still heavy. Despondence seemed to prevail all around me. Dejection tempered my spirits like malaise. Little me wondered if there was any place for me in this world. What was in store for me? Dark clouds seemed my lots and there appeared no silver lining.

Meeta, patient with me heard my anxiety like a good listener. Encouragingly she persisted and tried to instill a positive point of view. Seeing one so positive it seemed such a contrast to me.

"OH, nonsense! You'll never do anything if you don't persevere. Now why do you think you failed?" All this year fate has been against me. First, I was ill with hepatitis, which lost me a month. Then just before my examination my father died and that upset me so much I could not prepare properly." "Well, well you certainly had bad luck. You must make up your mind and get through."

"The most interesting thing is that balance depends on one's frame of mind. Understand? Which means that if you are cheerful and firm in spirit, there will be more zest and nothing whatsoever will negatively affect you. But as soon as you lose heart, the potassium gains the upper hand and you may as well order yourself a coffin. This idea is sound. I am sure in a hundred years scientists will discover a protective salt that spreads over the organism if there is a clear conscience and dosen't, if there wasn't. And it would depend on that salt, whether one swims or sinks."

No, no, no it's no use, I was born unlucky. I seem to fail everything I touch; I tried several times to get a scholarship, but some other boy always got it instead. I am not a paragon of virtue, nor a Monolisa. I have nothing exceptional to count on. No outstanding qualities that will cancel my shortcomings. However, the wish to go on torment me. Though at this point, I feel like giving up." "Indeed, you must not. Remember it is the darkest hour before dawn. Failure is a stepping stone to success." But I can't believe in all this." "You have a year before you, if you pull yourself together and put your heart into your work, you will win."

My despair had been expressed. The weight on my mind was lightened. The turmoil which had been whirling, subdued. I seemed to float. The void seemed expansive; emptiness prevailed all around. Fate seemed to rule my destiny, and a fate totally against poor little me. Yet it won't speak to me, and tell me what the future had in store for me.

So much uncertainty, so much suspense. What am I to do? Have I nothing in my own hands? What will happen? Am I to wait patiently and accept my lot? I wish I had a hopeful disposition. I wish I had the power to break the so called bad luck. Fight with my fate and conquer it.

Life after all, I can't believe is so determined. The will of a person should lead him somewhere. It was circumstances that kept circling around and narrowing down on me. That despair, that black hopelessness naturally became me.

Yet, strange enough hope pushes me on.

ON THE MAT

Sahib's phone ....

She knew what he was about to say. "Congratulations!

New department!"

"What's wrong with it?" She snapped. (Too much on the defensive. Not showing a calm mind and control.)

Ashok did not expect such a reaction. At least, not this soon. "Did I say, there was?   Far from it. This is what you

needed. If you don't work for Women's Welfare, who will?"

Akansha cut him short "I have to hand over. I'll call you, later!"

She slammed the phone.

Theirs was a strong Indian marriage. Generally, happy too. The kind that that goes on for a long time without either of them muddling up. Working daily, at what they had. Growing in how they felt towards each other.

For now, however, Akansha had more pressing concerns. Her husband's (Ashok's) patronizing tones could wait.

Today, she felt an outcast. At the back of her mind, Akansha, as she tried to concentrate on the job at hand, was still wrestling with reason of her fall from grace. Casteism! Why, does it exist? Could the upper caste survive, today? She doubted it. If the chief minister had his way, he would send all the upper caste officer to teach in primary schools. Sixteen years in service and now this. Akansha, was competent. She didn't play politics. She had been in finance, heavy industry, public works, and appointments. Akansha had also been in charge of the hill district. Climbing the ladder when most of her women colleagues complained of discrimination. And, now this! The Department of Women's Welfare?

"What does one do – ", she wondered? Distribute sewing machines, goats and chickens! The cacophony of the assistants, not visiting villages! The seniors monopolizing all the vehicles of work. "Anyway" Akansha reflected, "it could have been worse!" This job would at least enable her to get home early. Quite a blessing, after clocking ten hours at work most days, for so long.

On Akansha's third day at her job, Mrs. Manjari Jhorie, her Co-Director, continues briefing her with the problems within the Women's Co-operative. Akansha interrupts her, "How do you like the work here?" "Work? –Nothing works!? Manjari, the slightly bored, mildly annoyed government office, wincing and shrugging her shoulders with a familiar sing-song hum continued with her run-down of the Co- operative:

"Thirty five districts have been identified for various Women's Projects. As it stands, monitoring is impossible. Staff had not been posted in sufficient numbers. Statements, too, are always delayed and inaccurate. Nutrition for nursing mothers have been sold off. Women's groups are unhappy and no longer function". Manjari, heaved a deep sigh, "Production, is virtually at a standstill".

Akahsha, looking Manjari in the eye, bristled, "surely something has to be done," who too was desperately searching for answers to get out of this predicament. Thinking on positive lines, Akansha said "Staff has to be motivated". Manjri quickly added, "Heaven knows, we have enough meetings, workshops and seminars, keeping to government guidelines". She rolled her eyes. Tapped her biro upon her jotter. "Tons of pamphlets have been distributed. But, mostly in English. Our women have their own regional dialects, you know".

Akansha reminded her, "Staff has to be motivated for more efficient operation. When the turnover improves and they understand the benefits of pay-for-performance, it will spark creativity and strengthen efficiency." Manjari gave a light nervous laugh, "I have heard it all before!"

Despite her fresh light heartedness, Akansha, seeing Manjari's resistance, weakened. For a flash of a moment, she didn't want to stay on, in the department. Spending days, inspecting Women's Co-operative. Producing twenty pickle bottles each month. Was the way OUT. Or, else she'll be in a pickle herself. But, until then, her full attention had become a lifeline to the women looking towards her. Her vibrant self, got the better of her, "Manjari, I'd like to go to Varanasi on Saturday, visiting blocks. Inform the officers concerned please, regarding the projects to be discussed". Akansha was determined to make a difference, and to recognize a simple workable system.

With the news of the Director's proposed visit, the government machinery creaked into motion. The Assistant Project Officer, Mrs. Bhatnagar arrived. Years with the government had narrowed her focus, not to mention, placed her emotions on a short fuse. Now, it was anger strongly felt, with good cause, that Mrs. Bhatnagar kept her field visits to the minimum.

Moreover, she knew the inspection ritual a little too well. In all probability the Director would not arrive. In which case, they would all be lined up; and wait – until, the mystery Mrs. Singh, was officially announced. "On the other hand," considered Mrs. Bhatnagar, "If she did arrive, it would be worse! No doubt, having in toe, lavish snacks and non-existent local delicacies would of course, have to be arranged." And if, she did not, she knew, she would have to face the Almighty's wrath. "What are these things you keep? Don't you ever budget your finances correctly? Oh! What do you women do? Uoo la laah."

Mrs. Bhatnagar knew if she arranged the display of goods– demands would flood in. Five kilos of pickle for the District Magistrate sahib's memsahib. Hand-woven durries for the Assistant District Officer's bungalow– "Demand, demands, and more demands. All of which would never receive payment." But would Akansha do the same? Would she allow these demands? Did motivating employees mean this?

Mrs. Bhatnagar, pushed her thoughts aside as Anjana walked into the room. Anjana, was a frail woman. Seemingly tireless, and nearly always cheerful. Mrs. Bhatnagar acknowledged Anjana's greetings and briefed her about the Director's programme. Informing her that Akansha Singh had taken charge of the Department, she was competent, clean, smart, and in the Administrative Services.

So, attempting to be the professional-devil that Mrs. Bhatnagar was, she put just a little fear into Anjana. "As you are organizing most of the work here, be prepared....... Call all the women and make a list of problems". "Try and see", with an exasperated sigh, "not to make the list too long, or for that matter to complain– about me! Mrs. Singh won't come back. I am here to stay".

Anjana's cheerfulness momentarily left her. Her thoughts went back to when she started the small durri manufacturing unit. It would occupy her, and of course, add to the much needed income. A good part of her resources was being poured into the project, involving about forty women that made up the Durry unit. Now, it was co-operative. But, Anjana was the woman in-charge of purchasing, marketing, getting funds and taking durries to the different fairs. She often had to accompany Sheela to the bank. Helping with applications. Going to the tehsil, tracking down revenue records.

Somehow Anjana got involved with everything, it felt strange. She was to young when she married. Her husband was a good man. The only child of doting parents. They loved him so much. Anjana, their daughter-in-law was so happy. A pretty little girl and a child bride. They never let her do a thing. Except, constantly reminding her to wear this or that. Her husband never ever raised his voice. Every day he would return from work at five thirty. Take the children on his bicycle. Bring the vegetables. Then they would sit together and talk. Share a meal, eat and laugh. A happy life. And, then it happened? Her catastrophe! When no one could really help.

He died. Anjana's world collapsed. Just twenty years old. With a matriculation, three children, father and mother-in-law in failing health, with orders to vacate government quarters, Anjana was naturally at a loss. In fact, heated arguments with her dead husband, seemed the only option.

"Why………. why in all your years didn't you teach me? Never let me buy vegetables? Lift a heavy bucket?........

"I'm here", you said. Now, "Where are you?" Chasing your Provident Fund?............. Three years, everybody said, I could get a job. Word, more words…   I, ache all over.

Sitting in front of the Assistant District Magistrate's room, all day. Day after day, jewelry utensils all sold.

Though, not nearly enough for medicines, or food." Five

years of all this. Five long years, then finally the Provident Fund and later, a job as a peon in the tehsil. Her in-laws passed away.

Many problems were sorted, others remained, new ones focused. Everyone knew she lived alone with her children. No man in the house. Men in the neighborhood lusted over her. Other women felt threatened, wherever she went. Sometimes, Anjana wanted to die. Men still leered. Women still slammed doors on her face. Women, living along. Women without men. Even Anjana thought often, "Single women were entitled to dignity."

All over, all, in the past. The children had grown up. Anjana's gray hair and her work, finally gave her enough dignity to be invited to most weddings and be addressed, "Anjana Mausi", by the whole village. Along with a sense of happiness–a lot of it, this gave her a sense of responsibility which, Anjana needed, to feel good. An added purpose of wanting to 'DO' something with her life. Injustice, pained her – as it pained most others. Now, it angered her. Most of it wasn't even necessary.

Now, Director Sahib, would come and Anjana would tell her, "Everything", "But, would Akansha Singh have the time to hear all the nit-picking details?" That worried Anjana. She would write them down. Make a list. Akansha Singh, representing the Administrative Services, as Director, Women Welfare would put a word. Things would change.

Jerking back to reality, "Oh God". Anjana remembered, "the durries have to be cleaned. The women have to be told. So much work." Anjana panicked.

Akansha, does not look up or ask him to sit. "Yes, Madam", he begins, "block staff have been informed. It has been listed in your diary. It says you have visits to Rajapur and Raipur." Akansha, still doesn't look up from her desk. Thoughtfully, with mild annoyance, "I'm not sure. There might be a change of plan. I have to be in Varanasi all day, on the twentieth. Blocks must be covered in one day. No…, no………, one day for visiting blocks. Guptaji, would like to ask – "How?"

But, decided this wasn't the time. Akansha said, "I'll decide when I reach there". Guptaji's smile was telling. Seeing again, what he had seen so often before awkward, grotesque pride. Such arrogance that accompanies every small fragment of power even in an improvised society.

"No Madam", Guptaji knew he had won hands down, in his concealed king-pin position. "You will not decide. No one does. You will simply do what you please. What is convenient to you. You will inspect carpets, lovingly, and mentally picturize this one, for the sitting room and that one for the guest room. Have a leisurely lunch. Then, suddenly you will remember you had to go to Rajapur? Or, was it, Minat? The phones won't work and the women will wait." Patient women, with children. Women with sparkling bottles of spiced pickles and carefully cleaned hand-woven durries. Women, with long lists of complaints. They will have to wait. Guptaji smiled sweetly, bowing, hands folded, in the Indian custom.

Did they have to wait? Was the story to be repeated with Akansha? Sometimes the call of duty is strong. Stronger when marked with commitment.

TOO GOOD TO BE TRUE

What a beautiful garden! The seasonal and the perennials all arranged, and flowering. A small nursery in one corner of the garden. Winter in full bloom. Chrysanthemum, dahlia, and not to miss the multicolored gladiolus. Oh, the spread of fragrant roses abounds. This was her passion. The spread in front of an antique residence. The back too had a lineup of seasonal vegetables. Making herself sufficient with the daily quality of vegetables. Whose was this hand behind?

"Get out, get out" the landlady ran behind, stern and serious. He rushed into his room expecting her to follow, what may have happened then? However, foresight and providence kept her. "Oh, do not create a scene in front of the gate' came the retort. She stuck to her ground, "Oh! get out." "I need my things." He runs into the garden and digs up the nursery, takes all the treasures yet to come. She sits helplessly watching the devastation, not knowing what to do. Yet adamant he gets out.

Finally, he goes and with her hair standing she walks in. To avoid going crazy she continues her daily work. What really happened? Why this burst …. why this anger? Yes, he had come two years back to take care of the garden.

When in six months the garden looks up, and his request to spend more and more time was granted until finally he shifted in.

Oh, that was some judgment.

It was over a year and he was trusted beyond the garden. He'd do odd jobs to please—Can I get anything from the market? Would you like some milk? There are fresh fruits down the lane. Oh! why are you sweeping? I'm there. You've been working so hard. Let me clean the house for you.

It was too good to be true.

One morning while working on the table came a request, may I have the broom? No response, so a little louder— Give me THE BROOM. Go take it and he entered the house for the broom but doesn't return. Getting up from the table she goes to see what happened. There he was with his pants fallen and the man in him awake.

Without thought, poor man, he receives gifts of clothing which probably provoked an unknowing situation. Other left over foods and clothes soon became gifts. Poor person, what a pain. On narrating this incident to a friend, the danger loomed large. However, this incident had taken place. It was in the past, so no action could be taken. In addition, to wait for repetition was dangerous, however, it was not far behind.

Often without realizing, he sat hours without speaking just staring. Pleading to be taught, 'please teach me English'. Somehow, discomfort made her shut her doors and work. However, he stood behind the shut windows she couldn't imagine why. Once on a hot day, he comes rushing—Oh! It's a hot day can I stand under the fan?   Oh, please?

…… walking into the study. All right, the woman walked out. Then on thinking what cheek, how impertinent. He has disturbed me. Why doesn't he go into another room, she goes back to the study? The realization wasn't two minutes, when she walked back. Low and behold, there was the MAN. Oh! Get out of here. GET OUT.

Was that to be the end? Yes, Providence what more do you have in store?

Every time she went to the main gate, he stood there like a lamppost keeping check, morning, noon and night.

Open the gate, there he is going to receive someone, going to see off, lock up for the night, no respite. From just standing and staring, it became sitting with a notebook keeping a record of all who came and went with vehicle numbers and how much time spent. As if that was not enough, the moment the gate was locked for the night, he would lie down and sleep for the night.

Oh! How difficult, the woman does not notice, in comes a bouquet of fresh, handpicked choicest flowers. In addition, in the neighborhood, "Oh, that cruel woman, she's not giving me the rest of my belongings." Plea's came from neighbours, inquiring about the matter, requesting to take him in, explaining it's human to err.

A trying phase, oh patient woman, afraid, tortured, not knowing how to handle the situation. Pained to think how long it will last, and what will follow. How complicated life can become, all for no reason. How to sort out this mess? An unnecessary complication, very unimaginable.

However, one day the woman had a male visitor. This lamppost was as usual at his post. When the visitor was seen off, he approached and accosted him. The visitor, in shock, was silent. However, the woman knew it must end now. She locked that gate and went into the house contemplating, feeling miserable; to break the misery the phone rang…………. Hello?...............Oh 'He…

Why are you sounding so frightened? In your own house? I'm just coming over. No, no, no, I can't open the gate.

Come on, I'm coming.

Within ten minutes there was a bang at the gate, hesitatingly she went to the gate and asked, "Who's there?" Open. Your friend with the inspector. The gate was opened, he was pointed out, interrogated, forced to clear the room of his belongings by the inspector, armed and in uniform. Threatened of being handed over to the police if seen in the locality.

Yes, the job completed, her friend left. She once again locked the gate, feeling uncertain not knowing what would happen. The words 'get out' rankling.

The Pioneer Lucknow Thursday 19, 2002 Reported: BURGLARY

A case of burglary was reported from Wazirganj locality. The report stated that miscreants broke into the house and ran-sacked 8 a.m. to 12 noon.

STYLE: 2004

In tears lies this story. Tears of joy, tears of agony, tears of grief, tears of remorse. Yet we can still smile and keep going on, no matter how wretched our lives can be. Someday the reality will be in the open.

Madhu, young at twenty-six, ready for her first assignment. Fresh and straight out of college. Skeptical from experience but prepared to take up the challenge. Oh yes, very much a master mind. Yes, three long months and a guest to someone she never knew, but the organization promised her free board and lodging. And she was determined, I'll take it though the assignment doesn't provide.

Confusion, the first night in a strange city, I ended up sleeping in the rear seat of a car parked in a hospital ground. The next morning at work, everyone had to know, the tears and more tears. The sympathetic boss recommended her strongly "keep her like your younger sister," not realizing how difficult personal relationships are and cannot be built overnight.

Oh! What a relief, I have somewhere…however, no confidence, so I take my fiancé's friend to check out. They drive me down. In order to get out of the tight situation they approve off where I was putting up. If nothing the proximity to them; who'd never turn up to keep me out of the way.

As if their responsibility was over. Yes, the assignment had promised me board and lodging.

Yes, she's acknowledged by others as Aniha, though unacknowledged by myself. Her middle age gives birth to her surrogate ideas and to nurture them, she ends up mothering and thus become stepmother to myself. Nevertheless, she's not as complex and confused as it sounds, plainly not as simple as her looks permit others to think, she's free from herself but not from her ideas, from the society but not from its complexities, from the past but not from the present. Therefore, that is Aniha. In addition, she housed me for three long months. Her deal was no rent.

I accepted and she was happy, without knowing what was in my acceptance. However, I made most of the situation, and was determined to save on lodging, and much more. "Oh, Aniha I'm full, I won't eat today." – "I've cooked, would you like to taste?" Then that was Madhu's chance– 'Gorge' sometimes a week's foul flesh. All down in a meal, not even a morsel for the worker. "Oh, you know, from childhood I've loved non-vegetarian food. I can't resist, I just end up eating till it's all over. As if there will be none for tomorrow! Mother said I was like this during my childhood. Old habits die hard."

This continues, I request, ask and finally become demanding. "Oh! let us have mutton today. My diet chart says 500grams of chicken per meal. I wish you'd cook it, you cook tasty stuff, and with it, I'm allowed rice too. Oh! You are going to fetch milk, a packet for me too. The washer man's come; can I give my clothes too? I need a kilogram of apples; will you get it on your way back? Oh! where, oh where will it come from?"

Oh! All my life I've watched TV all the time. No movie would I miss. Aniha had TV, but she'd never use it. Maybe she watched news occasionally. I'd love 'City Radio' on all the time. I would love sound, reaching the remote end of the world. Oh! how I missed TV! However, I'd get to it movie time on Saturday and Sunday and till the rest of the world I am watching. Oh! yes one day I wanted to watch a movie, and didn't want to pay. What was I to do? I talked Aniha to come with me. When it came to buying tickets I just moved away. Oh! How wonderful Aniha paid for both the tickets. I invited her, I recommended the movie but being younger, it was my right, so I made it to a free movie. Maybe I'll manage a few others.

Then came a teaching assignment outside the city. I'd never done one before. I planned we'd do a workshop. But how was I to manage? So, I trapped Aniha, made her plan, made her get all the material and finally, saying we'll to the session together, watched TV and look full advantage of hospitality provided by the host organization. Wasn't that the way it was to be? In addition, that was my final achievement. I am going to use that material all my life. Moreover, I will take great care, Aniha is nowhere on the scene. Won't that be some achievement?

Yes, weren't those three months' good? What a good experience. As if that was not enough, the next semester I returned with more vengeance. Aniha in the meantime had asked me to shift out. I couldn't imagine why? I, was good company, young, beautiful, ready to accept all favors and enjoy a little spoiling. Oh, it's all in the game, a phase of life!

NO PAINS NOGAINS

Life's ugliness is realized too late, when life's broken, all sacrifices made and love turned into habit. New illusions are needed for one to go on living. All right, then look at that huge three-storied house down the road.

It's Sunday, isn't it? The time's morning. The washer man has arrived with his weekly wash. Rinku is emptying out the pockets of Nitin's shirts and trousers before handing them to the washer man, when suddenly she discovers that letter. A crushed and crumpled envelope addressed to her.

Rinku's whole system seemed to be on fire. She sat down on the bed and took the letter out of the envelope; her eyes went to the date. It indicated that the letter had arrived three days ago. She turned to the postal seal. It confirmed the date, Nitin had opened it, read the letter, crumpled it and shoved it into his pocket. He did not even think it necessary to let her know about it. The fire within her reached blazing point then, and pervaded every nook and corner of her being. This was certainly not due to forgetfulness; it was a deliberate act. This was his habit.

Nitin kept the key of the letter box with him although they were a joint family with fifty pairs of hands–pardon a little exaggeration. Usually he read Rinku's letters and then passed them on to her. Sometimes he did not care to do that.

At best that was her conviction.

To tell the truth however, till now, there was no proof that Nitin had opened her letters. However, upset Rinku loses her temper with Nitin. Flings harsh accusation at him and castigates him in unthinkable terms, but to no avail. Nothing works, her alternative strategy, talking gently to him falls on deaf ears. In the beginning he used to make light of the whole thing, then when his patience failed him, he too lost his temper.

Rinku sat quietly for a few seconds in order to calm herself, then read the letter. It was from her mother, nothing serious. In her usual manner her mother had listed her troubles and difficulties, adding that the ceiling was leaking. It needed repairs urgently, or else it would give away and she would die under the debris. However, she felt her daughter and her generous son-in-law would not allow that to happen.

Rinku's mother was poor and widowed. She was able to get her daughter married into a rich family because of her daughter's beauty. But the mother never failed to take credit for arranging such a match and always took advantage of her prosperous daughter. When her mother's letter came Nitin would comment, "Don't waste your time reading it. I had better fill out a money order form."

Rinku wanted to die of shame. Only the other day she had written to her mother telling her not to write, on post cards. She had decided to send money to her secretly without Nitin's knowledge. Now there was the result of the letter sent in the envelope. This made Rinku terribly angry like a --------.

Why did she put her in his awful position all the time? No, this time she was going to let her mother know that she would not be able to help her anymore. Please do not expect anything from me now on.

At that moment Nitin entered the room. He had just had a bath, he looked refreshed. Rinku's simmering rage found its victim now. She roared like a tigress. "When did this letter arrive?"

Looking askance at her, Nitin realized the seriousness of the situation. Actually, he had decided to tear the letter otherwise it would mean some more money wasted. As a matter of fact, he did not want Rinku to know that a letter had arrived from her mother. What a mistake. He had completely forgotten about it.

But Nitin wasn't going to give in that easily. He pretended not to remember, "letter, which letter?" And then, suddenly as though seeing a light he added, "Why, of course, a letter did arrive from your mother."

"I didn't find time to give it to you, sorry." "Why not? Why? Why? Tell me why didn't you give me my letter?" for goodness sake I forgot, that's why? "Liar!" hissed Rinku, like a snake. "Why are you calling me names? Don't people forget".

"No, they don't. Why did you open my letter?" Nitin tried to make light of the issue. So what? My own wife's letter." "Shut up. I repeat. Don't lie. How dare you open my letter. Haven't I asked you a thousand times not to." Nitin wasn't afraid of Rinku's temper as much as he dreaded a scene. So, he smiled weakly and said. "What if you forbade me to? Don't I have to check if anyone is writing love letters to you." "Stop it. You are mean and despicable."

It would not be fair to expect Nitin to continue smiling even after this. He angrily said, "Why indeed, only those who write whining letters to their sons-in-law are well born.   A poor girl has become a queen, I suppose." "Shut up", shrieked Rinku. It was a blessing that their room was in the third story, there were many in that house who would have enjoyed eavesdropping. "Shut up!" growled Nitin. "Why should I shut up?" "What I say goes." "Can't I do anything? nothing at all?" Rinku panted breathlessly. "Do you want to see what I can do?"

What Rinku did I cannot say, because at this junction her niece Rani came on the scene. "Aunty, how long will the washer man wait? If you aren't going to give any clothes, tell him so. "She picked up the clothes and calmly replied, "Tell him that I am coming in a minute to give him the clothes."

Seeing Rinku, her sister-in-law said, "Thank God, at last you found time to come downstairs. Really, any excuse to be with your husband. Aren't you two ever tired of talking?" "Have you finished preparing the vegetables?" Seeing the burnt end of sari, she said, "Oh! How did you do that Rinku?" Rinku pulled the basket of potatoes and started to peel. While peeling, her thoughts were preoccupied with how to send the money to her mother.

However, women have enough within them to start a hundred major fires, but they don't flare up to burn the mask of nobility of their men. They don't explode their own colorful calm, exteriors. That's why men let them be without any apprehension in the kitchen, in the living room and in the bedroom here, there and everywhere.

SELLING HER SELF SHORT

There Was A Flood Gathering Flock at the EXPO 91. Predominated by Women, Highly Self-conscious, Intelligent and Rational. Their Eyes Wandered Form Patolas, Pochampallis, Chanderies, Kotas, Tangails And Daccai's. Bewilderment Hung All Around, Some Fascinated, Others Shop, Shop, Shop Till They Drop, Drop Drop.

Crowds spread over the park like waves. From among them emerged a young woman looking beautiful and confident, her rather uncertain husband by her side in a mental flux imagining himself confronting the cashier. A young child following.

Seeing the splash of colour all around, he resigns to a position under a tree near the cafeteria for refreshments while his wife satisfied her curiosity. He has been given instructions that he was to be sent for to face the cashier of the stall if she made any purchases.

So, she went from stall to stall with the words of her spouse.

"Mind you, take care and don't be rash in choosing", said her husband.

"Take a good look at all the stalls first and then decide. Don't get lost. When you decide to buy, send the child for me. I'll come to your rescue."

Knowing all the while, that he held the reigns of the purse, "All right", said the woman, "I won't take long," and she proceeded. The husband, more relaxed, sat with a cold drink, and happily puffed away at his cigarette.

While she and her child strolled from one stall to another, encountering the sales staff, making them miserable, pulling out everything in the stall, opening it up, without a word, leaving the sales staff confused and irritated with all the prices repeated and re-repeated. The sales staff consoling themselves–Wisdom is in learning to overlook; and I am wise, if that is WISDOM.

After this attitude is repeated at a few stalls, her feminine nature gets the better of her. "Oh! How can a woman contain herself with just feasting her eyes and not yielding to the desire of a good bargain?"

She walks into a stall; her eyes are immediately attracted to a beautiful baby-pink chanderi. The cost, to her mind, appears reasonable. She begins to consider. Then, orders the salesgirl to empty all the shelves, spending all her energy and time explaining the authenticity. "This is a very beautiful hue, exquisitely sober, just the thing in vogue and well in keeping with the weather. Formal, to greet an evening get-together with elites. The material has a natural sheen. And the final leash a 20% discount. Take home at half the actual cost. First, a government enterprise, unusual, a variety, not so easily found in Lucknow.

The convincing arguments of the salesgirl, somehow gives her temporary encouragement. Mentally tapping her resources, she is aware of the fact that her husband is waiting under the tree. She sends her daughter to fetch him. "Papa, Papa, please come. Mummy has chosen something she wants to buy."

Irritated at the prospect of being disturbed, add to it a possibility of having to pay a bill sends Mr. Arora following his daughter to the pavilion. Fully armed, aware of his wife's nature Mr. Arora enters the stall seeming rather interested. But on hearing the price giving a very condescending glance. "A soft pink, isn't it beautiful?" she adds in the most winning tone. But, Mr. Arora retorts, "Don't you have so many in that colour? Moreover, it's a colour for the young. But of course, whatever you say, it's the wearer who counts." Mrs. Arora realizes that the eye of the beholder is not satisfied. She is slightly disappointed. But she strolls out leisurely followed by her husband and Kushe. Totally indifferent, feeling victorious Mr. Arora decides to walk with his family from stall to stall. Smiling, he lights another cigarette.

On entering the West Bengal pavilion, a beautiful Tangail holds her attention. Encouraged, the prices being reasonable once again the racks are emptied. The customers feed their eyes on the displayed variety.

This gives a cool comfortable look, especially with the approaching summer. This time she gives it a serious consideration. The salesgirl perceiving her growing keenness takes interest in her customer and dances to her tune– "This piece is exquisite. The hue of grey and vermillion has given a rich blend. This is the only piece with this extraordinary combination. Summer is around the corner and the sari is most becoming. It will add glamour to the wearer."

Once again Mrs. Arora is tempted. A smart salesgirl from the other counter walks by, "Oh! How elegant that sari looks. If it is not bought off, reserve it for me." She ponders for a while. The smart salesgirl insists "Put it around you, see the effect, look in the mirror" while she drapes it. "Just gorgeous" remarks a passerby. Finally, confident enough she looks for her husband who's standing by her side lost in his own world. Till she impatiently pulls at his sleeve and says – "I want to buy this sari. What do you think about it?" Quickly, as if planned, another person walks up, admires the piece and in a flash has bought it and stalked off.

In the meanwhile, Mr. Arora, annoyed and ruffled, is convincing Mrs. Arora who appears displeased with what has happened. The idea of adding another sari to her ever- growing wardrobe does not appeal to him. He subtly argues "Tangails are for slim ladies. It won't suit you. Besides, you should go in for something more exclusive, something which can be preserved till posterity." She insists at least, look at it. When she asks the salesgirl for the sari she is told, "Madam, it has been sold." With a heavy heart she leaves the store.

Mr. Arora sighs with relief. Consolingly he tells her, "Try at another stall, you may have better luck this time." She feels rather cheated, her heart was set on it. He muses to himself "Women and sari, the Expo is making them crazy; one would imagine they haven't seen the like".

Mr. and Mrs. Arora once again start their march from stall to stall. An air of determination in the stride of one, and an air of disappointment in the other. This time she enters a silk pavilion. The stall is artistically set up. To greet customers is dashing young, smartly turned out salesman. A salesman who is as indifferent as he is smart. Naturally, more gracious to his younger customers. She overhears him repeating from customer to customer. "Pure silks, the best variety   in prints, forty to fifty grams costing Rs. 230, the sky being the limit after a twenty per cent discount. Exclusive prints, exquisite, always in vogue and adds to the grace and charm of the wearer." Despite the commercial edge in his voice he attracted ample audience. Emptiness of the situation began to grip her. Impulsively she wanted to be the centre of his attention. "Show me that sari please, what does it cost?" She asked politely.

"What variety of silk are you dealing with?" The salesman totally disinterested, working mechanically answered-

The causal air he had picked up, the effort he had so far put in, seemed to have drained him totally. He was exhausted.

But consoled himself, saying, 'It is an exhibition first and sale next. Displaying and explaining is part of the game". However, by then Mrs. Arora having seen a large variety selects one, admires it for a short while. His silence somehow disturbs her, feeling, conscious that no attention is being focused on her, she recedes into the world of saris that surround her, and means to make a selection, taking time deciding, so that this time, there is no chance for refusals.

Mr. Arora quite irritated, at having to spend a neat six hours at the Expo, reminds his wife that they other commitments. 'Time's up, we must go home." "Come back tomorrow, it will be easier to choose." This message hits her. She expresses her confusion in an audible murmur.

"It bewilders me he doesn't see me."

PART- II

TO DAUGHTERS

My daughter once asked me Mom, "What does 'a good life' mean to you?"

After asking she continued to ramble that she and her friends had a long discussion. They wondered if a 'gap year' was necessary to think through. Instead of going straight from high school to college and then straight into a career rat race, there must be an unstructured time of exploration. A friend said her parents feared a gap year may disrupt a student's momentum, but can't it be part of the momentum?

After listening patiently, to a young view of a good life, which meant financial success. It is naturally a focus on money and power. But as one grows success is not only that. The question we need to answer for ourselves is, "Was this the life we wanted?", or "What is the life I want?" Is it simple to answer at an initial stage in life? However, somewhere along the line we abandon the question, and shift our attention to how much money we can make, how big a house we can buy, how high we can climb on the career ladder. Those are legitimate questions, particularly at a time when people are still attempting to gain an equal seat at the table. But I painfully discovered, that they are far from the only things that matter in creating life.

Yes, overtime my notion of success was reduced to money and power. In fact, at this point, success, money and power had practically become synonymous in my mind. This idea of success can work, or at least appear to work for a short time. But over a long term, money and power by themselves are like a two-legged stool – one can balance on them for a while, but eventually you are going to topple over. And more and more people, very successful people, are infact toppling.

For success one has to go beyond money and power, so that there is some balance. Which means we redefine success. And the price we pay in terms of our health and well being continues to rise. Work culture has a lot of stress. But there is no ban on after hours work which is a clear signal, we can. But in some places, it earns us overtime. The danger of work culture, built stress, leads to burn out and constant dissatisfaction.

The stress of our business, over working, over connecting on social media and under connecting with ourselves and with one another. The space, the gaps, the pauses, the silence those things that allow us to regenerate and recharge, had all but disappeared in our life and other lives too.

People who are genuinely successful in their lives are ones who have made room for well-being, wisdom, wonder and giving.

Hence, the third leg of our stool brings balance in life and makes life truly successful. Do we give back after our first inning?

Well, you need to think on these issues, may be in your own way. What do you want from life? and as you go along your views too will change. However, what I've said is my way of looking at my life today?

See, in my case the work place culture is filled with stress, sleep depreciation and naturally burn out. Stress undermines our health, the deep deprevation is profoundly and negatively affecting our creativity, productivity and our decision making powers. Where is the time to think, to recharge and to rethink, or reconsider? Very often, isn't it required.

For me, the biggest issue with work has been fatigue not pay. At the cost of pay we sacrifice our bodies and mind to work the long hours, it takes to earn money not to mention the stress. The lack of sleep effects our cognitive functions. Sleep deprevation reduces our emotional intelligence, self-regard, assertiveness, sense of dependence, and empathy towards other this effects the quality of interpersonal relationship. Our positive thinking and impulse control too may be hit. In what gets better with sleep deprivation is "negative thinking" and reliance on superstition starts.

For me success means not only building and securing our financial capital but also protecting and nurturing our human capital. More often our stress is due to our sense that there's never enough time for what we want to do. Don't you think "We are more than our resume's. Our resume gives what we have done. But what about the 'real me', the quality of the person. Eulogies: citation, applause, compliments are not you the real person, it's some one's perception.

Remember, we are a part of all we have met. The millions of little judgements that emanate from that inner region. To reconnect with ourselves in a word is my meaning of a "good life."

I BELIEVE

Loneliness isn't just being secluded from others. It's ______

being around people that make your feel alone or suffer in silence. Maybe, feel misunderstood or just not at the same wave length. The possibilities of mental and physical distress shared, you're stigmatized or judged. This simple end up in 'You' withholding your true-self from those who surround you. Unconditional acceptance, is rare. However, we should listen to understand and not to judge.

S.J. (Facebook post)

'One' is not a lonely number. A number of people live alone, and this number is growing. Does it mean single households are isolated, or does it show loneliness is increasing. Being alone and being lonely are two different things.

Single households can be home to the happy loner who actually both needs and enjoys having a lot of time to her or himself. There is the contented solitude of the creative artist. And there are many who relish rational periods of solitary life.

The opposite of loneliness isn't popularity either _ you can have dozens of 'friends' be the life and soul of every party and still feel that deep disconnect that is the red flag of loneliness.

Much of isolation that we see in society today comes from people spending time every day with so many different people, all of which required intense activity for brief periods. None of the contact is very substaintial or meaningful.

The criterion for loneliness therefore does not lie in the externals, the number of social engagements you have, how many people you interact with during your working day , it lies in what you feel inside. It's about feeling isolated, it's about an inner most need for human contact, loneliness is caused by some factor or another in particular circumstance for instance it can be age related, genes, marital status, belief in God and individual perception. However, people with anxiety depression or other mood disorders admit being lonely.

Sometimes sleep is where one de-toxifies the stress of the day. Loneliness makes sleep less efficient. Sleep disorders may be due to different reasons, but loneliness undermines the body's quintessential restorative process. Very often lonely people suffer from terrible depression, chronic pain, and/or fatigue. These occur in clusters and are mutually reinforcing; it lowers the quality of life and long-term survival.

It is a vicious circle, and one needs to break out. But breaking free and overcoming this trap will mean acknowledging it. Many people are in the denial mode. They resort to numbing the inner void one way or the other. They might watch Tele, travel the malls, surf the net, hangout, or use drugs as a crutch. Or they might try to keep busy and superficially engaged in life, immersing themselves in chores and activities. But sometimes none really work.

One should therefore, acknowledge this lonely feeling and become aware of its repercussion. Your loneliness in fact serves as a crucial signal that your relationships are not as emotionally close, supportive or engaging as you would want. So, it offers you a chance to identify this problem and make efforts to fix it.

One must try to figure out what's missing. Yes, fixing loneliness is about getting more connectedness in your life. But the question then is, what kind of connectedness, and how do you go about getting it? The short or the simplest answer may be friends. But when and where do we find these friends? Friendship is not about numbers but quality of your relationship. A few quality relationship – deep rich relationships, may be that is what it takes to get out of the grip of loneliness. Or may be doing something that give you value. The worth lifts you and gives happiness.

Even without structured activities or opportunities. There are times you feel connected. Try not to plunge recklessly. Take it easy. It's important to realize what is important.

The negative thinking needs to be cracked down. As it is a self- destructive cycle. So, make the leap, with a serious effort have the courage and faith to escape. Is it always so simple?

This mystery called happiness cannot be rationalized. It is a subjective, positive experience of enjoyment. This internalized feeling or emotion is in varying degrees for different persons. How do I come by it?

How does it come?

Happiness is a mystery like religion, and should never be rationalized.

It is subjective positive experience of enjoyment, and internalized experience, varying in degrees.

BALANCING LIFE

Sheela tells her friend Neela that she is anxious and life is very difficult. She is unable to make a headway. Neela listens to her patiently and finally tells her to try and find a balance, by deciding her major goals. Maybe once she is clear in her mind about what she wants she'd be focused and in less stress.

Life is all about finding a balance, Neela suggests, in anything and everything we do. A balance between friends and family. A balance between fun, work, education and home. A balance between doing for others and doing for oneself. However, is this simple? Can it always be possible? How do we go about doing it?

Neela says if something feels wrong just do not do it. Intuition does not come to an unprepared mind. Remember the intuitive mind is a sacred gift whereas a rational mind is a faithful servant. Today we have created a society that honours a servant more than a gift. To identify pure intuition, listen to your body and the signals it's giving. Try developing a focusing practice that allows you to achieve a calm, detached state where you can better identify what is going on. One needs to distinguish between wishful thinking and projection in intuition. It can be a feeling in your gut. A nagging thought that won't go away. A strong feeling you get about something.

This specific emotion innate to us as humans is our intuition. We possess this capacity to feel, and thereby have the ability to know without reasoning. This 'gut feeling' is real, and we unknowingly use it at all times. Though going with our gut however implies uncertainty. Whatever you call it gut feeling or inner voice or sixth sense intuition can play a real part in peoples decision making. Intuition is non conscious emotional information from the body or the brain such as instinctual feeling.

She continues to emphasize that one should say exactly what one means, speak your words with power. Speak your truth and say what you feel. Meaning what you say is not being a hypocrite, once said assume your words as your truth. It's a circle, if you say what you mean, you can mean what you say. Giving and receiving honest input is important. Listen and reflect, accept and respond. Stay in the moment and don't quit. Sheela feels it's very difficult.

Neela tells Sheela that she should just stop pleasing people and be a people pleaser. People pleasers are like a breed of dogs or a nutritious salad which is immediately filling. This intense need to please is deeply rooted in either fear of rejection or fear of failure. Fear of rejection comes from abandonment or inconsistent relationships. Whereas, fear of failure is the underling feeling that if I make a mistake, I will disappoint people or be punished. It can lead to significant anxiety. And this can be a back log. Regardless of origin consistently putting others needs above your own develops negative consequences. Neglecting self becomes passive aggression and resentment. All this reduces the ability to enjoy, and leads to stress and depression, so possible taken advantage of, by becoming a push over. All this seems too complex for Sheela; however, she continues –

Do you know, I often blame myself if things go the other way? Speaking ill is self-blame. It is a process in which the individual attributes the stressful event to oneself. The direction of blame often has implication for individuals' emotions and behaviour during a stressful situation. This pulls you down and down.

Only when you can follow your dream does life look more meaningful. When you show courage in the face of adversity you change your life. The most provocative people in the world who won't settle for average and have triumphed through adversity inspire others. Luck is undoubtedly great, but most of life is hard work, and it is the only way out of stress. Always face the challenges to overcome, this is what struggle teaches us. Undoubtedly, it is much simpler to stay in your comfort zone and avoid risk. However great things never come from mediocrity. Quit settling for the average and strive for the extraordinary. One must find strength in stress, conquer fear and live your dreams.

Just say 'No'. There is nothing you hate more than doing something you just don't want to do. Sometimes we may have to work, do a job we don't like or do seemingly pointless homework for a class we are just not enjoying. But in circumstances and places where we do have a choice, we can say no. We should if that's what we really want. Why should one need to, or learn to give excuses? Why should one be afraid to say no. No one will think lesser of you. No one will stop wanting to spend time with you. There is no point dancing around the world. Just say 'No' and move on. 'No' is a painful word. 'No is a difficult world too. One may feel bad to say no, but 'No' sometimes is unavoidable.

However, say 'Yes' when you want to connect with people. Humans need to connect with each other. Building connection is all about understanding the people around you so becoming empathetic really helps. I build connections with good friends and groups of like-minded people. We connect to warm gestures. Though we connect to strangers through a cause shared interest and values. Our worst enemy is within ourselves. It is about being positive for yourself and others. You don't want people to suffer. Compassion and forgiveness go hand in hand. So, the mind has to be attuned in that way.

Carve out some time for yourself, and do something that brings you joy. You can draw, write a journal, write a short story, play a musical instrument or do anything you love. Be kind to yourself by giving yourself some 'me time' each day. Then give yourself recognition, become aware of your achievements. When you do something you are proud of, stop dwell on it. Relish your achievement. Complement yourself. Cultivate your inner advocate, we are all familiar with our inner voice. The inner voice which is quick to judge should defend you. Always forgive yourself. Sometime or the other we all mess up. May be there is some skeleton in your cupboard. Perhaps you failed to stand up for yourself and you let someone else get the better of you. You missed a great opportunity because you got scared. Maybe you failed to follow through on an important goal. Take good care of yourself. One of the best ways to show yourself kindness is to love yourself. Get enough sleep, eat plenty of fruit and vegetables, and get some form of exercise on a regular basis. In addition, choose a way to release stress, be well groomed and look after your appearance. In caring for yourself, you will respect yourself for who you are, and not allow others to dictate your value. It's trusting yourself, forming your opinion, and making your own decisions. In addition, it is refusing to compare yourself to others. Finally, self- respect is keeping your promises to yourself and following through. Once in a while treat yourself. I am not advocating a shopping therapy. However, if you see something you really want, treat yourself.

Once I really had a tough day. Well, it started out with an argument. Then the presentation went hay wire. It was just one of those days in which everything that could, went wrong. What was I to do? I sooth myself, returned home soaked in a warm tub, with aromatic bath salts. How good that feels. Or try a scalp massage, may be get your feet rubbed. Make yourself a coffee with a light snack, just enjoy a light book or movie. Lock yourself, turn on music of your choice and dance. It really works for me. Just give it a try.

Remind yourself of your good qualities, you are different. Lift yourself up. Tell yourself, 'I am enough,' We all have bad times in our lives, when we've thought, 'I'm not good enough' replace it with I'm enough, just as I am; I'm worthy, I deserve to be happy, I deserve to have everything I want. In this way honour your dreams. People who respect themselves respect others. They are kind to themselves so they do not downplay their dreams by labelling them as silly fantasies. Instead their dreams become their goals and they keep planning to achieve these goals.

There has to be a sweet spot between accepting and striving. Part of being kind to yourself is acknowledging your potential. Stop trying to be perfect, people who set standards of perfection for themselves are setting themselves up for failure. After all perfection is unachievable. Can one be unkinder than making success impossible? Instead show yourself compassion, believe in yourself, and accept yourself.

Oh my, how can we free yourself, by "letting go" of what we can't control. The paradox of control. The more we try the less control we will experience. The things you can't control will seriously disrupt your peace of mind. Learn how to let go as soon as possible. As soon as you make the shift of leaving behind your worries and stress, not wasting your energy on something that's not in your hands you'll be a whole lot happier. The only thing you have control over is yourself. You can take charge of your decisions, attitude and reactions and that's about it. So, learn to let go of some things in life, purely because they are not in your hand. For instance; everything in life changes, the weather, traffic, the past, the future, other peoples mind and other people's happiness.

No one wants to carry baggage. However, we see things differently. So toxic people should be avoided. If you have family, friends or even acquaintances who swim in a life full of drama, tip toe out, save yourself without looking back. You can't be a saviour, fix others issue, or continuously listen to negativity. Believe it or not, it doesn't really matter. As it will rub off on you and may even have a negative impact on you.

It is rightfully said you are who your friends are. And may be this concept is right. It is good to surround yourself with likeminded individuals. Which means, largely they should be people with similar interests, similar ways of thinking, feeling, reacting, communicating and having similar values. Don't bring people into your life who are constantly complaining, who are lazy, miserable never happy, never satisfied or who blame others all the time.

Love yourself enough to recognize a toxic situation or a toxic relationship and end it. You deserve to be happy. Therefore, you should make a conscious and definite decision to listen to grumpy and disgruntle people. Who because they are unhappy do not acknowledge their issues? Surround yourself with those who bring out the best in you, who lift you up, motivate and inspire you. Be with those who bring a smile to your face, laughter in your soul and recognize their own imperfections. Surround yourself with those who have pure intentions, no ulterior motives and who truly have your best interest at heart.

All of us want inner peace, alone time, space and even our sanity. We all deserve to survive with peace and calm, rather than in negativity. Go to sleep on a happy note, feel good, at ease and be happy. You will get up happy. There will always be one person you will have a relationship with and that's yourself. So, live your best. Neela leaves Sheela thinking.

YES, I DO!

Poonam married a man 22 years older, but now she often wishes she married someone closer to her age. Do you think she regrets it?

Her parents had major issues with it. They were not happy at all with her decision. "He was not only twice her age but also from a different culture, with a heavy baggage. Oh! Westerners pride themselves in their own unique identities. They like to thinks for themselves, and they value individualism. Whereas Eastern culture by contrast tends to be much more collectivist.

However, society looks at her as someone who married a sugar dad/dy or a gold digger. He was already successful, especially in the material sense. There was still a lot of social stigma surrounding the age gap relationships. What about the older partner's peers and they being judgmental their belief that such relationships are transactional relationships? Poonam had to grapple with this fact that he was much more established in a stable profession than her.

I'm a very type ' A ' career-driven person and feel like sometimes people look at me as someone who married a gold digger. There's this assumption that it has to be exploitative. People today say, 'Yes I do!' but I don't often feel that, they feel that way about this kind of a relationship.

"I had kids younger than I may be wanted to Poonam and Arnold were united on that fact that they wanted kids. But Poonam believes that, if she had married someone younger, she might not have ended up having children at twenty four.

Being with an older man definitely pushed me to have kids younger than my demography. She felt that people often looked at her asken once for having her first kid at a very young age. People in different places may be relatively open minded but I felt people gave the looks that said, "Don't you know how to use birth control?" Social stigma does wear you down. It's ideal if both have decided not to have kids.

People often mistake my children's father for their grandfather. "That causes him to back out". Poonam says strangers often assume Arnold to be her father, possible because this unequal age marriage are not uncommon but stigmatized. People often think he is the grandfather which is naturally a little uncomfortable for them.

"I was a lot less emotionally mature then I thought, I was when I got married." As, many women who marry older men also complain their partner's likes do wane just as they hit their prime, it is very much the case. For Poonam, he definitely has some disfunction issues though younger men have them too, but it's become more prevalent when you're older. However, looking back twenty years later she feels, how could she have got into this.

"I've never felt like I was in a relationship of equals. Arnold was old school in terms of male female roles than I would guess men my age. My mom says ' he treats the kids like a grandparent rather than a parent by being over indulgent and not as great with discipline". This meant a zero overlap in parenting techniques. Eastern vs Western parenting. Mother wants to shout at their children to discipline them. Small kids' small problems, bigger kids' bigger problems. On the other hand, dads will say, "you have been terrible behaved go and relax." "Here is Leo, go be happy."

"The man in the house makes a lot of big decisions because he's the man, and older, doesn't mean wiser. And he was already established in his career for nearly all my life which naturally didn't make it easy for me to build something of my own". "Therefore, the marriage was not of equals. Though I did not carry the burden of a financial responsibility. I've lived in a nice place. I've always had money to travel. And I have never been in a phase of living in a one bed room apartment and eating paneer."

"However, I will spend a good part of my life as an older person alone. Or spend a chunk of my life feeding him, ovaltine through a straw before the ultimate. The relatively short self-life of marriage. While I feel I might have been happier with a man closer to my age. I am not planning on anything. Marriage for me is very important as an institution because of my beliefs. But I have had to come to terms with the realization that I will spend a good part of my life alone."

Once the two live together the vast gulf in life stages emerge for examples if one person still wants to go out all the time and the other is in a phase of life where the other wants to spend more time at home can cause problems. One has grown up on Ravinder Sangeet while the other on Bach and Beethoven.

Where will that twain meet? There is bound to be conflict.

It's one thing to marry a Dad (father) figure who takes care of you, but it's another to ending up with a dribbling, old cranky wreck. Yes, everything that has a beginning must end. What do you presume the end will be?

DOMESTIC ANGELS

A woman said to me once so proudly, "My family never quarrels." and I thought "How wonderful! If only I could say that." But I know better. When I look back on a family who never quarreled, I remember their passivity, the slow eyes that never flashed; on the parent's face, no grooves that tears had scoured. I know now that it takes passion and energy to make a quarrel of the magnificent sort. Magnificent rows, magnificent reconciliations, the surging and soaring of magnificent feelings.

At its best a family can, be an island of acceptance and love in the midst of a harsh world. But too often within the family people take out on each other all the pain and frustration of their lives that they don't dare take out on anyone else. Instead of a readymade source of fruits, it is too often a readymade source of victims and enemies, the place where not the kindest but the cruelest words are spoken.

A 'lone person' can be happy, as I have got to the point of considering that there is no more respectable character on earth than an unmarried woman who makes her own way through life quietly, persevering, without a dad, husband or brother support. Who having attained the age of 35 or upwards retains in her possession a well-regulated mind, a disposition to enjoy simple pleasures of fortitude to support the inevitable pains, sympathize with the suffering of others and have the willingness to relieve want as far as her means extend.

I am, in truth, very thankful for not having married at all. I have never since been tempted. Neither have suffered anything at all in relation to that matter which is held to be all important to women, love and marriage. Nothing, I mean beyond occasional annoyance, presently disposed of. Every literary woman, no doubt, has plenty of importunity of that sort to deal with; but freedom of mind and coolness of manner disposes of it very easily: and since that time, I have been speaking of, my mind which has been wholly free from all ideas of love affairs. My subsequent literary life was clear from all difficulty and embarrassment – no doubt because I was evidently too busy, and too full of interest of other kinds to feel any awkwardness – to say nothing of my being then____ years of age. At which if ever, a woman is certainly qualified to take care of herself. I can easily conceive how I might have been tempted how some deep springs in my nature might have been touched, but, as a matter of fact they never were, and I considered the immunity a great blessing under the liabilities of a moral condition such as mine.

If I had a husband dependent on me for his happiness, the responsibility would have made me wretched. I had faith enough in myself to endure avoidable responsibility. The care of children would have overpowered the simple joys of life. The energy one needs to put in would have exceeded the ordinary chances of 'being'. The fear on my part would have impaired the freedom, that I can rejoice not to have been involved in a relationship for which I believed myself unfit.

The veneration with which I hold domestic life would probably be unjustified.

When I see what conjugal love is, in extremely rare cases, perfect. I feel that power of attachment or call it submission has never been touched in me. My strong will, combined with anxiety of conscience, makes me fit only to live alone. The older I have grown, the more serious. This makes the evils of married life irremediable. It is the bane of single life to in ordinary cases to want, substantial laborious and serious occupation. My business in life has been to think and learn, and to speak out with absolute freedom what I have thought and learned. This freedom is itself a positive and a never-failing enjoyment in me. My work and I have been fitted to each other. As has been proved by the success of my work and my own happiness in it. The simplicity and independence of this vocation suited my nature and sufficed my needs together with family ties and domestic duties such as I am blessed with as a women's heart required.

Thus, I am not only entirely satisfied with my lot but think it the very best for me. And I long ago came to this conclusion that, without meddling with wives and mothers, I'm probably the happiest.

OH! TEACHER

From our last conversation you seem to be polemic. This means you are associated with the teaching of "the conflicts". So, will you say combativeness is a deep personal motivation of your life and work. Conflict, struggle, bitter argument and long drawn out arguments have become a part of you.

Gautam: Yes, partly not entirely. People think I like conflict because I promote it as a pedagogical strategy. In fact, I dislike conflict. In odd ways my interest in conflict has been tied to a longing for community. However, I just don't think a democratic community can be sustained by papering over its divisions. 'Teaching the conflicts is a way to get beyond the conflicts. My assumption is that the more we avoid confronting conflicts the uglier they can get.

Anita: Can you explain what you mean by longing for a community?

Gautam: When I first completed post-graduation, I sought advice from my professor about the "profession". "The great thing about this job" he said "is nobody bothers you" what an ambition for a professor – not to be bothered! And what a community in an institution that calls itself an academic "community."

It is the isolationism of the academic ethos that I have always disliked and struggled against, both in my work and in my personal life. That's why, after years of being a solitary professor I jumped at the chance to become a department chair and later a university press director mostly just to have someone to talk too.

Anita: But aren't you exceptional in seeing this as a problem? Gautam: Well there are others for example Dr. Sunita, Dr.

---, Dr. ----- and many others. The university is dominated with an "ethics off alienation and aggression", that has bred isolation and professors are estranged from their colleagues on campus and from communities in which they live.

Anita: Yes, surely there is plenty of "community" on campus 'black studies' 'woman studies. 'neo conservatives" Gandhian studies 'and 'disability studies' all sorts of groups.

Gautam: Yes, these communities lend themselves to be isolationist. All too often groupings which form within departments are within fields actually functioning as anti- communities, small coterie's who band together as much as to ward off outside influence as to foster collaborative work. Such scholarly anti-communities are essentially defensive in nature a bonding by which an insecure sub group tries to gain a sense of self-worth at the price of learning from divergent views.

Anita: It seems academics cherish their isolation as much as you say, how would you hope to change things?

Gautam: Academics is often tremendously ambivalent about the pleasures of isolation that they cultivate it why else have academic conferences and symposia become pervasive if it isn't that they answer to a longing for community that isn't being satisfied by their home campus? You can sense this longing in the hyper excited atmosphere at such events, suddenly for a few days. Here are people you can talk to, about your work – metonym in the Elizabethan lyric, or cross dressing in the Eighteenth century, or what your will. These are conversations you aren't likely to have at homebecause anybody who shares your interests is probably by definition disqualified from being your colleague.

Equally pathetic is the abyss of local silence and indifference into which we academics send our publications. When we publish an article or book, we'd think our departments or colleagues would look for an occasion to discuss it publicly. Instead the "publishing scholar" is made to feel almost embarrassed about committing a public act even if he or she is rewarded at salary time. Again, when you go to a conference, your publication becomes a reference point, but to make it a reference point on your home campus would be like provoking your personal life.

Anita: Why do you think these academics "ethics of alienation and aggression" has taken root, if in fact it has?

Gautam: The "insecure" status of the academic sub groups that bond together against the threat of outsiders. Academic culture is grounded in insecurity and fear – as environment could be, where rules are revised all the time. That no one is sure where one stands wherein fact revising the "paradigm" before your competitors do it is the name of the game. Students fear professors, those distant and unfathomable beings whose arbitrary laws change from course to course without notice, professors fear students who can humiliate them by their mere silence and passivity; professors fear their colleagues as their rivals and competitors. The university provides no institutional arena for discussing these fears out in the open, they get channeled into self- protective behavior.

It's all well and good to talk of "community". But wont such a community seem coercive to those who like their privacy or isolation. Yes, no one is denying privacy. It's just not understandable why universities are organized around who wants to avoid having a discussion.

In a general community a doctor wants his/her child to be a doctor, an engineer wants his ward to be an engineer, a civil servant wants his child to be a civil servant but what about a teacher. Why does a teacher want any of the above?

No one wants to be a teacher by choice very sad, but that's the truth. MS Anita had a reputation for honesty and frankness replied after considerable thought. You want to know what I make?

Well, I make kids work harder than they ever thought they could. I make kids sit through forty minutes of class time when their parents can't make them sit five minutes without an iPod.

You want to know more! Anita paused again and looked at each and every person.

I make kids wonder.

I make them question.

I make them apologies and mean it.

I make them respect and take responsibility for their action.

I teach them how to write and then I make them write. Key boarding isn't everything.

I make them read, read and read.

I make then show all their work in maths.

They use their God given brain, not the man-made calculator.

I make my students from other countries learn everything they need to know about India while preserving their unique cultural identity.

I make my classrooms a place where all my students feel safe,

Finally, I make them understand that if they use the gifts they were given, work hard and follow their heart they will succeed in life. Moreover, all students listen to those who make a difference, spread positivity, give hundred percent of themselves, stay organized with an open mind, who uphold standards and embrace change. More than everything they destress students and treat them with dignity and respect.

LOOK OUT

One afternoon two friends were walking from the Botanical gardens through Saharaganj to Tanishq. On the gate of Sahara Ganj, one felt her left leg was caught and took time to move forward. However, she finally went on.

An uncomfortable feeling persisted so she looked down at her leg half way in Sahara Ganj. The legging seemed torn. So, she went on to reach Tanisha. The discomfort kept nagging. So, she went to the 'ladies' and saw the teeth marks of a dog's front teeth. She was shocked. The blood had dried. She immediately told her friend. If a stray dog bites you, do you know what to do?

Both rushed to a near-by hospital. The wounds were cleaned. But how? With water and soap or Dettol/ antiseptic and cotton swabs. Yes, a lay man says plenty of water and detergent. However, water too, today is not pure. Practically every home has antiseptic, if not, always keep some in reserve. Well, after the cleaning got an anti- tetanus injection. And then was advised to got to the closest government hospital.

The most important is to get anti rabies injection, within twenty-four hours of the bite. A one-time shot is 'Human deployed vaccine' but not available despite the search.

So where is one to go? Naturally, and as suggested to a government hospital. Yes, when she did go to the government hospital. It only had rabi pa, not in the freezer. Oh, my and its severe side effects. May be, even a stroke. She pays for the series of injection, she gets the injection and then she has the possibilities of side effects anytime, anywhere. This surely doesn't appeal.

After much cogitation, consulting doctors and friends. The one common suggestion that emerged was to go to a vet. But once again a vet specially deals with animals. No doubt we are higher animals, but why a vet? The other suggestion was to consult a pediatrician. That was undoubtedly a better suggestion. But you mean dogs don't bite adults? We did contact a pediatrician. He agreed to start the course from the next day. At least that was well within twenty-four hours.

Guess what that night when she changed for bed, the churidar that holds good memories was removed, she discovered the back of the calf had the marks of the lower teeth in the mouth. They were less deep but the two canines were deep. Probably they were the ones smarting. One can well imagine the entire mouth had left its impression. Now a life time sign she will carry.

The next morning accompanied by a friend she reached this child specialist's clinic. He suggested she get a be-rab which was to be used on that day and then the same injection   at different intervals of second, fourth and eleventh day. Together with be-rab to get a Rabi shield, which was for each tooth mark. Aah! imagine the pain.

Oh! Why take so much pain for no fault of your own. So, be careful, watch where you put your next step. Is this providence?

A CLEAN ESCAPE

On an unusual Sunday morning life appeared beautiful to Reema. All the morning chores completed be it cleaning, washing, cooking or anything that suddenly pops up. She was ready early enough to visit a friend, Nisha to return for her special Sunday lunch.

A pleasant sharing of the frailties of the week, made them decide to have lunch together. Reema, soon returned home, lunch over, so her special stacked away. After a good lunch what does one do? So, she changed and planned to relax for a while. While relaxing she just got up and walked into the garden. The weeds she had asked her gardener and overseer to clear caught her attention. The tall pine was encased in the largest size money plant leaves. A creeper weed had overtaken the entire trunk.

That was the provocation, she started pulling it down. Reema from her lawn started, one by one to pull the shorter and lighter tendrils, which kept getting pulled till she felt a sense of achievement and so she continued. But soon she came upon a stubborn stem and pulled harder and harder, and finally with all her strength. Can you guess what happened next?

Oh, the impact – it flung her backwards till her back hit a pillar made of mosaic – it was solid – Multiple thoughts flooded her mind soon. "She was gone, her hands and legs seemed so lifeless, was it total paralysis?" It took a long two minutes to get movement in the fingers and then the hands. That was some relief. It did give her courage. She finally crawled to the bedroom and lay on her bed for half an hour.

Despite all the thoughts racing in her mind, she realized she needed the phone, and contact a doctor or a friend. Gut told her to contact Parul who could scale the main gate. Reema told Parul she had fallen and couldn't walk to the gate.

Naturally, Parul living at a distance took half an hour to reach. In that half an hour Reema got slow walking back with a lot of pain in her lower back. Parul came with Stella and Zara her two daughters and a driver who could climb the gate.

Well, well, Reema reached the gate in slow motion, and opened it. Rushed the kids off to the pharmacist to get 'iodex' and 'move' and then applied the first aid. After resting for some time, she went for a drive to test if she could sit.

The drive turned out longer than she could handle so it became painful. Oh! For the speed breakers and the pot holes on the road. This gave her the idea of how sitting could be in office.

That night and several to come that followed once she lay down, Reema could not sit up or get out of bed due to the pain. So, the shirking and the shouting. The memory of that pain remains in her mind even today.

After the weekend Reema was more comfortable at work, sitting the duration of the work hours and driving too and forth.

What an eventful Sunday! It left its mark for weeks to come.

FOOD, FOOD AND MORE FOOD

For Maya

"Please season it as you think fit. A failed effort to make Labra! But it is edible" D.

A revolution, knocks on the door, and it comes with a fork and knife. The world of food is more exciting than ever before. New restaurants are coming up offering novel cuisines or digging out old ones. Chefs are looking at unusual ingredients and dramatic ways of presenting food. Meanwhile, some wisened old experts continue to wield magic with their skewers and ladles in remote parts of the city. There is a world waiting to be discovered or remembered new cooking styles, world food, sub-regional cuisine and tiny holes in the wall which produce the most delightful dishes.

Festival times you will hear an interesting medley of kitchen sounds: one sizzling hum of fish being fried, the grind of mustard seeds being turned into paste, the sharp sounds of onion and garlic being grated and the splutter of seeds in hot oil. For this is the time when cooks and kitchens get especially busy.

All festivals in Bengal are about food. A meal comprises of a dollop of rice, small wedge of lime, various kinds of fritters and a dry vegetable. Then in bowls go the special dishes; lentils with fish head and Labra/shokto, and mutton in thin gravy, fish cooked with mustard, prawns in coconut milk, chatni, curd and papar. And, not to forget a platter of sweets.

There was a time when all this could only be had in Bengali homes there really was no restaurants.

Today some of these dishes have been given a makeover.

The five top favorites:

Topshe cutlet a small fish, eaten fried. The de-boned fish is fried in rice powder till it is crisp. Maachher dimer devil_ deviened fish roll spiced with garlic, onion coriander and coated with gram flour and fried to taste. Amada dry lau ghonto (bottle gourd with mango and ginger). The table does not lay only meat and fish, there is an equal array of veggies, whenever there is a feast, starting with stuffed parwal to chopped bottle gourd. Lau ghonto is a bottle gourd preparation cooked with mustard oil, salt and sugar. Add some raw mango and ginger for a kick. Look at Kancha aam duya bekti patori (steamed bitki with raw mango). The banana leaf works wonders too. Though mustard oil and mustard paste are the main ingredients, raw grated mango adds punch Khulna chingri curry, this is a variation of daab chingri which is a shrimp cooked in a whole green coconut. A little red wine added to the coconut base make the curry fly off the plates.

What about the traditional mixed vegetable Labra? The uniqueness in this veggie curry comes from the addition of few. It simply elevates any dish. With the combination is a lip snacky chutni prepared with tomatoes.

What about winter, let the mercury dip, the frenzy in the kitchen goes up by several notches. It's not the regular three meals a day, it's the sutradhar (chief chef) that binds the family and the larger circles. A few of the must buy staples.

Korishutir Kochuri is a seasonal specialty this is stuffed loochi with fresh winter peas. But it's not that simple. This can be eaten as a snack or with a potato curry. Then you can have Patishapta, this is a kind of crepe stuffed with Khoya and patali/nolen gur. Then the patali_gur_payas, essentially a rice pudding. And why not fish fry with different batter. The fillets being marrinated according to choice.

Oh! Why won't we always think of food. Isn't it just delicious, will one ever want to eat out? No, no, no.

SPECIAL MEMORY

As Jai dropped into his swing chair near the brightly burning fire his eyes rested on a large photograph of Eva. The young girl, Eva had given him forty years ago. With a sense of awe, he looked at the frank forehead, serious eyes and happy innocent mouth of the young creature whose soul's custodian he was to be. That terrifying product of the social system he belonged to and believed in, expected everything looked back at him like a stranger.

It was born in him that marriage was not the safe anchorage he had been taught to think, but a voyage on an enchanted sea. Though a culturally recognized union. It establishes rights and obligations between two people It is a spiritual and emotional union, which can have its turns and twists.

The case of Eva, with her shy and different appearance, hid the steely grit. The photograph had stirred up old settled convictions and set them drifting dangerously through his mind. His own exclamation, "Women should be free – as free as we are", struck to the root of a problem that it was agreed in the world to regard as non-existent.

"Nice" women, however wronged, would never claim the kind of freedom he meant, and generous minded men like himself were therefore in the heart of every argument –

Such verbal generosity was a disguise of conventions that tied things together and bound people down to the old patterns. But here he was pledged to defend, old beings. Of course, the dilemma was purely hypothetical since he wasn't a nobleman, it was absurd to speculate what his wife's rights would be if he were _ _ _.

But he was too imaginative not to feel that in his case and Eva's, the tie may gall for reasons far less gross and palpable. What would he and she really know of each other, since it was his duty as a decent fellow to conceal his past from her, and hers as a marriageable girl, to have no past to conceal? What if, for some one or the other reasons that would tell with both of them they should tire of each other, misunderstand or irritate each other?

He reviewed his friend's marriage, the supposedly happy ones and sure none that answered, even remotely, to the passionate and tender comradeship, which he pictured as his permanent relation with Eva to be ideal. He pre supposed, on her part, the expiring of versatility, the freedom of judgement which she had been carefully trained not to possess and with a shiver of foreboding he saw his marriage becoming what most of the other marriages about him were. A dull association of material and social interests held together by ignorance on the one side and hypocrisy on the other.

It did occur to him that his friends, other husbands, understood his visionary idea of a wife. It was so completely his own and undoubtedly convenient, that in case of trivial affairs what would transpire? She would go about smiling unconscious, with her original blush and averted gaze. That is when someone in her presence alluded to the fact that he had 'another establishment'

However, he add Eva would have lived in another world. As he was not an ass and Eva not such a simpleton. The difference (would be) was of intelligence and not of standards. In reality they lived in a world where the real thing was never said or done or even thought but respected by a set of arbitrary signs.

I over think, I over love, I over trust.   Were they ever together?

NOBODY KNOWS THE REAL ME!

The real me, The real me, The real me!

Oh! The pain backed with anger, regret and guilt takes many years to wash out. But what about the devastation the person concerned experiences, no one else can understand. Is it plain withdrawal? Is it simply isolation? Or is it the thought life is redundant?

Should one have the ability to overcome these problems? Recognize it and try to help themselves or is it too difficult. Why did their friend, spouse or sibling take their own life? Even a note explaining the reason is found, lingering questions remain. Yet they felt enough despair to want to die. Though the family did not feel that or see it coming. Ramesh's suicide came as a surprise. It took his family left behind standing still. It created a sharp pain in the members of the Gupta family. A pain of guilt for failing to see it approaching. To be the support system needed for their son. Life with its nuances had just swept them away.

Ramesh, nobody knows the thoughts that have gone through my mind; who had survived earlier suicide attempts had reported wanting not so much to die as to stop living a strange dichotomy but a valid one nevertheless. If only some in between state existed, some other alternative to death. I suspect many suicidal people would take.

We thought Ramesh was depressed. This is because without question, the most common reason people commit suicide is severe depression. It is accompanied by a pervasive sense of suffering. Suffering was for me a belief in hopelessness. The pain of my existence made me severely depressed and there were times when I could not bear it. This state wraps my thinking, allowing ideas like, everyone would be better off without me, though it hardly made rational sense. However, Ramesh shouldn't be blamed for falling prey to such distorted thoughts any more than a heart patient should be blamed for experiencing chest pain. It simple is the nature of the problem.

Depression is treatable, but we need to recognize its presence in ourselves and in our friends. Often people suffer with it silently, without anyone getting to know. As it makes both parties uncomfortable inquiring what happened. Suicidal thoughts in my experience always have weird responses. Nobody knows how many times I sat in my room and cried. How many times I have been let down?

We depressives are called psychotic. We have malevolent inner voices which often command self-destruction for unintelligible reasons. Psychosis is difficult to mask. Whereas depression is more tragic. The worldwide schizophrenia is round one percent and strikes otherwise healthy high performing individuals, whose life's and thoughts are manageable with lifelong medication. These people talk freely about their voices commanding them about thoughts of destruction. Psychosis too is treatable and must be. However, with drawl can have

Its repercussions. Was Ramesh's case a sudden with drawl of the medication? The process not being maintained or gradually stemmed.

Ramesh may just have been impulsive. May be it was an addiction to drugs or alcohol which crushed his inner voice. Substance abuse and the underlying reasons are generally a great concern and should be addressed aggressively. Often medication that is addictive and suddenly with drawn can also create problems, which takes you to any extent.

Posibly, Ramesh was crying out for help, and no one heard. No one had the perception or could see it. His anguish went unheard. It is only after the action that one could see the slips or the cues in the past. An incident comes to mind where Ramesh was invited and as long as he was present the mobiles went on. Naturally tearfully he questioned, why was I invited? If there was no time for me while I was there. Did it make him feel redundant? Or the continuous call make them appear larger than there were?

Nobody knows how many times I had to hold back tears. How many times I've felt I'm about to snap? Did Ramesh make a mistake. Then it was extremely tragic, and with no return. It is not easy to understand that depression is not a personal failure, rather a state of mind that demands sensitive professional care. In this fast-paced life, which has so much stress, anxiety and is unpredictable everyone gets depressed at some point or another. The wounds suicide leaves in the lives of those left behind by it are often deep and long lasting. The apparent reason of suicide fuels the most significant pain.

The demon is always within,

The goddess is always within,   Thebattle too, is always within,

So is the triumph of one over the other. The question is which one, over which one.

That choice is somewhere within,

The real me, real me, real me.

Part- II

LOOKING BACK

May I go home, please? Oh, come on, you always want leave. Three consecutive half days? Where you actually needed ten days for the sesquicentennial celebration's of your alma matter. Isn't this intrusion in our personal space?

Doesn't this say that the unstated rules of 'personal space' needs knowing, understanding and viewing it from the others point too. Within the office boundaries should it be observed? Professional distance and reserve are required. The inability to maintain and manage one's personal space generates invasion at a highly emotional cost. Seated 10 am to 5 pm facing the wall, just two and a half foot away (table space) reminds one of school punishments of 'stand in the corner', so irrevalant.

We are all made of experiences, likes, dislikes and ideas. Personal space is the buffer space that allow you to focus on yourself and the things that uplift your soul by being YOU in your personal space.

Workplace culture has changed drastically too because of this need for personal space. People are now demanding a work stations, where they can focus on the job. Are the office spaces being designed keeping the new requirements in mind?

If not, the employee needs to protect personal space at work, or we are likely to feel drained. "You may often feel hurt and angry for what seems like minor infractions. Infact the need for space is important that even intense perfumes in closed places, being sprayed all day may be intrusion when another colleague in office claims I love male perfume? Do you realize what you are doing to the others? Antagonizing, putting people off pretty quickly. In fact, the need for space is so important.

We are all learning to communicate. Social media has altered all our perceptions of what's considered rude and what decent. For instance, if someone adds you on his/her Facebook, Instagram, is it okay and to keep sending you message, saying "hi", or "I really like your smile?" Some may consider it just another way of communicating, while others will be very uncomfortable, even angry with such message. I personally consider it invasion of my privacy.

Another thing that comes up is, how do we navigate our personal spaces in an extremely public world? Can we, should we put posts describing our everyday lives, and expect our personal space not to be invaded at the same time? Personal space seems, is no longer the immediate space that surrounds us and moves with us. A text message is within the prism of our private space. But the danger is that it can be hacked by anyone. Because of this constant intrusion in our 'smart' lives we now have to fight for personal space much harder than it being the reason we want alone time, to block intrusion in our lives.

What is this 'personal space'? Have you ever thought about it? It may simply seem physical space immediately surrounding someone which they regard as theirs. Most people value their personal space and feel discomfort, anger, or anxiety when their personal space is encroached. Human space effects behaviour, communication and social interaction. It is the non-verbal communication including touch, body movement, paralanguages and structure of time.

The 'Hidden Dimension' or interpersonal communication is valuable in evaluating not only the way people interact with others in daily life but also the organization of space in their personal and official lives. It remains a hidden component of interpersonal communication that is uncovered through observation and strongly influenced by culture.

Undoubtedly, interpersonal distance of people is in four zones, intimate, personal, social and public space. And each of us look at it differently. Is the age factor or personality more important? Has modernity compressed these zones?

Entering somebody's personal space is normally an indication of familiarity or intimacy. However, in modern society, especially in crowded urban communities, is it difficult to maintain this space, when in a crowded train, elevator or street, one would think, however, what about choice of movies, talking and watching Big Boss, or even, Sephora & Nyikaa shopping and trying out in the office rooms where no one else is interested. How about the all day hunger-pang-peri peri, chicken popcorn, wings, biryani, name it and its on your work table Oh my. Many people find such physical proximity to be psychologically disturbing and uncomfortable though it may be a fact of modern life. In an impersonal, crowded situation even an eye contact tends to be avoided.

Then what about confrontation is that permissible? Not trying to see the others point of view? Is only my view, right? Oh, the demonstrations and confrontation, I am the favoured, come with loud expressions of anger. Why not, for once anothers perception.

Even in crowded place, preserving personal space is important. The amygdale is suspected of processing people's strong reaction to personal space violations. Amygdale, the structure in our tbrain responsible for telling us where the limits of our personal space lie. This structure is associated with fear regarding our survival instinct, so naturally a goodbye. Amygdale may mediate the repulsive force that helps to maintain a minimum distance from toxicity.

A person's personal space is carried with them everywhere they go. It should be the most inviolate form of territory. Body spacing and posture are unintentional reactions to sensory fluctuations or shifts, such as subtle changes in sound and pitch of person's voice. Culture and environment are factors which effect variance in communication.

Personal space is a 'hidden dimension' which does help reduce stress, and can help you stay focused, enhance your productivity, personal development and effectiveness who takes care of it? With, the present situation of 2020, it will become a new norm, a way of life, and more naturally accepted.

HELLO STRANGER

As the Shatabdi pulled out from Lucknow, I was happy and relieved to note the empty seat next to me, when a pleasant- looking lady came and asked me if she could sit on the vacant seat. I usually dose off during journey.

But this time, I had no such luck. I happily engaged in conversation through the journey. We talked and talked so much that both of us were surprised when we were in the outskirts of Delhi, time had just flown.

She went on:

If I have learnt anything from life, it's that sometimes, the darkest times can bring us to the brightest places. I've learnt that the most toxic people can teach us the most important lessons; that our most painful struggles can grant us the most necessary growth; and that the most heart breaking losses of friendship and love can make room for the most wonderful people.

Moreover, I've learnt that, what seems like a curse at the moment can actually be a blessing, and what seems like the end of the road is actually just the discovery that we are meant to travel down a different path. I've learnt that no matter how difficult things seem, there is always hope.

And I've learnt that no matter how powerless we feel or how horrible things seem we can't give up. We have to keep picking ourselves back up and moving forward, because whatever we are battling in the moment, it will pass, and we will make it through. We've made it so far. We can make it through whatever comes next. All this I learnt from life experiences. Married at eighteen, two kids in arms, and the sudden loss of the bread winner of the house, I was left at twenty two fend for myself and the kids. Spent a lot of time accusing life and destiny but had to grow up to give my kids the best.

The lady admitted, a bit abashed that she had done most of the talking and shared some personal moments of life too. Sheepishly she said she had told me some things she had never shared with anyone. But it did not bother her at all. Infact she seemed happy having spoken at length. It's often the ability to talk, feel comfortable and say what you think is important to you. We did not need name or numbers. There seemed no need to connect.

Remember growing up with warning against talking to strangers the first time you travel alone. However, this was a thought provoking encounter with a stranger, me being a good listener. It is believed, interacting with stranger one feels happier, as some secrets may be interesting.

People's mood improves and they, both the speaker and listener feel happier on the day they interact with a stranger. Even a brief talk with a stranger can sometimes help boost your sense of well-being and your outlook on life, and this sometimes leads to a deeper connect.

There is unexpected momentary pleasure in talking to strangers. This can lead to special closeness and "fleeting intimacy" It can comfort us as well as leave us feeling somewhat fulfilled and content. It is easier to communicate with strangers because we do not expect to meet them again, nor do we have any biases against them. So not fearing any consequences, we tend to open up and be honest, sharing secrets as well. Quite often, a secret begits a secret which leads to a warm interaction where you don't even expect a judgement with our defenses down and sharing can lead to rare insight. Is it any wonder that so many books, movies and songs revolve around encounters with strangers?

However, not all interaction with strangers may turn out desirable. But it is important to take the precaution of figuring out that you do not end up sharing your thoughts with a wrong person. It's our perceptions and maturity, that will help us to make the decision.

VOODOO, WITH LOVE

If the sounds of my waning mind could be heard, there would be a steady stream of questions. Did I lock the door? Did I shut off the gas? Is the CCTV camera on? 'What if' pops into my mind more often than I would like. Fortunately, I have a four legged teacher who helps me to get past my anxiety. His name is Voodoo. He is a yellow Lab grey hound mix. Who lives in the moment, has finally won over this struggling human?

On Sunday morning, I thought of taking him to a water park for animals. To let him exhaust some pent up winter energy. I thought it was a great idea until I started anticipating all the dangers that awaited.

What if Voodoo saw a bird? He took off after and never returned. What if he ran into the water and got poisoned? After all there could be dead animals that had poised the water. What if, Voodoo disturbed a small dog in the water, and the master came shouting.

After plowing through my lists of concerns, I continued on the trip. But the closer I came to the park the more worried I became. Still I had to smile, when I turned around to the back seat of my car and saw the goofy grin, on my furry teacher's face. Voodoo is no dummy. He knew exactly where we were going. He seemed to be day dream about long uninterrupted sprints in the water, jumping through the white frothy waves, created. Running and catching the Frisbee. He must have been looking forward to his latest water dance.

I started thinking of Voodoo's view of life and came up with a new set of what ifs. What if I have a good time watching Voodoo frolic? Instead of me being focused on what could go wrong verses what could go right. What if I took my camera out of its bag and snapped some fun action shots? What if I enjoyed myself too? And, what if I applied this more relaxed attitude to other areas of my life?

The closer we got to the water park the more excited Voodoo became. His joy was so contagious, that it infected me.

After we piled out of the car, I watched Voodoo going down the part and break into a smooth run, that happens when there is plenty of runway. He was a joyful carefree sight to behold. I captured the rest of the unfolding day through my camera lens.

After the film had developed it thrilled me to see that the photos said it all. It showed Voodoo plunging leap into the water, with his ears pinned back by the wind, and a happy grin on his face. This vision of 'freedom' reminded me of the life he taught me that day. Live joyfully and for goodness sake stop worrying. Life is far, far too short.

Well, well make the most of life. What will be , will be.